First Paperback Edition, 2010
Published in Canada
Book design and art: D.Grîn

ISBN: 978-1-926617-13-8

The Unwelcome Guest

plus

Nin & Nan

by

Eckhard Gerdes

Acknowledgments

Two sections of *The Unwelcome Guest* have previously appeared in literary journals in slightly different form.
"Worms of Wisdom" appeared in Fiction International, and
"Cities" appeared in Hayden's Ferry Review. The author
thanks the editors of those publications for their support
of his work.

Portions of *Nin & Nan* have previously appeared in literary
journals in slightly different form in other publications.
"The Sign" appeared in Blatt in their on-line Blogspot, "A
Pied Piper Arrives" appeared in Golden Handcuffs Review,
and an earlier version of the novel appeared in the Bizarro
Starter Kit (Blue) anthology published by Bizarro Books.
The author thanks the editors of those publications for
their support of his work.

Dedication

The Unwelcome Guest plus Nin & Nan are dedicated to my sons Sterling, Ludwig and Ulysses for their unwavering love and their support of my writing.

The Unwelcome Guest

The houseguest who was welcomed through the front door but leaves through the back has obviously been up to no good.

He'd been my guest for two weeks before I had an inkling of what he was up to. If I could find him now, I'd teach him a good lesson, but he's disappeared.

Other than his raspy and stilted way of speaking—imagine Foster Brooks impersonating a stoned hippie—the first mannerism of his anyone would notice was his apparent lack of control over his gestures, like the teacher in Sherwood Anderson's "Hands."

To some extent I understood his idiosyncrasy—"It's not easy being apparent," I'd once told him. "It'd be easier to be invisible." Some of us, though, take our responsibilities a little more seriously than he did.

The first time I'd heard of him was in Dubuque. I'd been running errands with my two youngest sons. After stopping at the hardware store, we began walking up the hill back towards the house. Jackson, the elder son, asked me why we had left the car in front of the store. I'd forgotten that we'd driven. We returned to the store, but I didn't see my gray Camry anywhere.

"Here, Dad," said Alain, pointing to an old red VW Beetle.

"That's not my car."

"It's Mom's. You borrowed it. Remember?"

Sure enough, my key fit into the ignition, and we were off, driving up the hill before I'd noticed that the sideview mirror was askew and the front windshield was too dirty to see out of.

I rolled down the window to fix the sideview mirror and must have crashed because the next thing I knew was I was lying on a bed and being attended to by a physician.

I wasn't in a hospital, though. I was in a diocesan office of the Episcopal Baptist *Chruch*. I saw the diocesan secretary standing to the side behind a long counter.

The doctor addressed her and said, "I've got a foot we can attach." I realized I must have come apart in the accident and that he was piecing me together. I also knew that I wasn't alive yet.

When the doctor left the room and the secretary was busy, I found a pen and a book on the nightstand. A name came to me. I had to write the name down before I forgot it. I tried writing, but I had poor control over my hands and fingers, and what I wrote was illegible. I turned the page and tried again. My "L" looked like an "F," and my lines overlapped. Still illegible. I tried a third time: "Edwin L. Thoth, Baptist minister." That was all I had time for. The secretary looked up just after I'd put the book back.

"Do you know an Edwin Lawrence Thoth? A minister?" I asked.

She didn't seem very shocked to hear me ask a question. "Let's see," she said, opening a filing cabinet. "No—the only Thoth in our diocese is a woman. Do you want her information?"

"Could he be in another diocese?" I asked.

"I'm not sure. Our national registry books are all out of order. I've been working on them with my assistant."

I was sure that part of Edwin Thoth had been surgically attached to me. I had to find out.

I'm not sure what happened next. I found myself walking on a beach and spotted something on the ground: a two-inch-wide political campaign button that said, "Hall for President." I assumed it meant Gus Hall, the old communist whose running mate had once been Angela Davis. I picked it up and clipped it on. It was in perfect condition.

Then I pulled back my shower curtain and found my cat inside the shower. "I should rename you Shower Liquor," I said, which was ironic—the cat's name was really Whiskey. I'd let Edwin name her that.

"That way when you're calling your cat, your neighbors will think you're a desperate alcoholic," he'd said. I'd been drunk enough at the time to find his suggestion amusing and to go along with it.

Eckhard Gerdes

My wife and I brought the kids to their grandparents and went shopping downtown. We had been drinking as well and stopped in our favorite three-story bookstore. Lotte left me in the atlas section while she went to use the washroom. I waited for a long time before becoming concerned. I thought I'd look around for her. Then I saw Edwin. I thought that perhaps Edwin had frightened her and that perhaps she was outside waiting. The alcohol befuddled me, though, and once outside, I lost my bearings. I sat down on a bench to clear my head. Not until the doors closed did I realize I had climbed aboard a bus and was sitting on the bench behind the driver. He demanded a dollar and seventy-five cents from me. I had to give him a five because I only had that and a ten on me. And of course, bus drivers carry no change: the money all goes into those stupid machines.

I guess I fell asleep. I woke up at the bus terminal on the north side, near Wrigley Field. I could hear the game. I knew I had to get downtown again to find my wife. However, I couldn't figure out where the return busses left from. Plus I needed change. I found a little drug store that was still open. In order to get change and directions, I bought an *Aquaman* comic book. The store turned off its lights as I left, and I saw a streetcar passing in front, heading the right way. I caught it and climbed aboard, paying the exact fare. I must have fallen asleep again. The streetcar stopped miles from my destination. I grabbed the bag with my magazine and got out. I hailed a cab for those last few blocks. In the cab, I pulled out my magazine, but instead of *Aquaman,* I had some lousy Italian fashion

4

magazine. Someone else must have accidentally taken my magazine while I was sleeping in the streetcar. When I arrived at the bookstore downtown again, I called home. My wife was there, safe, and said I should take the train north and then transfer to the bus home. I figured I could do that so long as I didn't screw up. If I got on the wrong train or bus, I might never make it home. I threw the magazine into a curbside garbage can and began walking to the train station.

When I arrived at home and began explaining my getting lost to Lotte, she did not at first hear me. I heard Jackson mutter, "It was Edwin's fault." However, I had not mentioned Edwin. How, I wondered, did Jackson know Edwin? Perhaps I had misunderstood.

"What did you say?" I asked him.

"Nothing, Dad," he said in his usual dismissive way. None of them ever talked to me about anything serious. They saved that for their mother. I was just the overgrown playmate. She was the confidante. Sometimes I really resented that. Other times I was glad for not having to deal with pre-teen angst.

Twenty years ago I published my first novel. Its characters included Viking-like cold-weather circumpolar people. One of these was a self-absorbed creep named Stambler. When I ran into Edwin in the grocery store one day, three years after I'd figured I'd washed my hands of him, he bored himself back into my attention and confronted me by stating, "I'm Stambler, right? You based Stambler on me."

That was untrue. Stambler was a fictional creation, as all my characters are. I told Edwin that, but he laughed it off and said, "Of course he's me. He's just like me. You must have based him on me."

I told him that at best my character may have been a composite formed from real acquaintances and imaginary types, and that perhaps he was in part one of the composite characteristics. I didn't think that was true, but I was trying to extricate myself from this confrontational conversation, this "duelogue," as another friend called such talk.

"I knew it," he said, walking away convinced of his position of privilege. I did not know then that I'd just made an enormous mistake. I did not know then just how diabolical Thoth would become.

He claimed to be a relative of one of England's Prime Ministers. That, of course, was also a lie.

The chair of my division, a squat Bulgarian fellow, told me I had to deliver two 100-gallon drums of hazardous materials and lone large wardrobe-sized carton from our warehouse to the business across the highway from the university. I asked him whom specifically I was to deliver these to. He said, "You're going to have to go in there and act as if you're the Chancellor. Don't ask. Tell them you're the Chancellor and you're dropping these off."

I was used to the chair's mistreatment (i.e. micromanagement) of me. He'd demoted me to the smallest office in the building, a windowless closet across from the bathrooms. He inspected my outgoing mail and monitored my phone conversations. He had his secretary rebuke me for using expensive paper for notes and for not leaving notes on my door if I'd left my office during office hours in order to go to the bathroom.

In a work climate where one's bowel movements are monitored, anything is possible. He'd asked me to schmooze rich wives of university system Regents in order to make him look good. He'd happily exploit my reputation as a novelist for the university's benefit, but woe to me if I sent a query letter to a publisher on the university's dime. So being asked to move a couple of haz-mat barrels wasn't that surprising.

The warehouse was a god-awful mess. I'd worked in warehouses before, and what was clear was that here as in all aspects of the university, operations were run by the incompetent. He pointed out the barrels and carton and left me to them.

They were buried by carts of books, dollies filled with unopened boxes, and loose construction materials. Unloading the carts by moving their contents to the shelving units took forever. The warehouse held more books than Barnes & Noble. The boxes were endless and were stacked incorrectly, sometimes precariously. I found large boxes atop small ones atop large ones atop small ones. Invariably such a stack would fall over and its contents—usually books—would split the corner of a box and tumble out. I'd have to unpack those boxes and check their contents against the packing slips because I wasn't going to be accused of mishandling the warehouse materials. The penalty for that would be a semester of only freshman composition classes, of extra committee work, of hideous outside social obligations.

I was finally able to clear a swath wide enough to move a forklift through, and after that, moving materials became easier—I palletized them and lifted them against a blank wall.

When I got down to where the haz-mat barrels and wardrobe carton had last been, though, they had disappeared. Someone had taken them. I was dumbfounded and no doubt would be in enormous trouble. I decided I'd be better off not returning to my office, so I continued to rearrange, neaten, and organize the warehouse for the remainder of the day.

When the time for leaving arrived, I made my way down narrow walkways and along catwalks in order to avoid the throng of faculty and students, particularly the chair. I decided to leave my car in the faculty parking lot and to take the train instead. On the way, I realized I had to see a man about a horse, but the only washrooms I was aware of were in the shopping mall above the subway downtown.

The washrooms there were cavernous. The unpartitioned urinals were packed together so tightly that one had to rub elbows with one's neighbor while letting go—if one could overcome such self-consciousness in order to let go. And shaking off the last drops would elbow such an assault on one's neighbor that fights would break out. The doorless stalls, the few that were there, were so narrow that one couldn't spread one's knees. The stalls were also so urine-soaked from those with bad aim that one's pants, when dropped to one's ankles, would soak up the collected urine du jour.

All I needed was a urinal without neighbors. The first washroom had a waiting line. I went to the next floor. There the men's room was out of order. I thought of using the ladies' room instead, but their line stretched out the door.

The third floor men's room was also overcrowded, but I waited my turn, and, as luck would have it, a stall opened up. However, as soon as I began to unbutton my fly, a gruff voice behind me swore at me and said, "If all you're doing is pissing, go to the urinals, asshole." I buttoned up and left. The fourth floor had no washrooms at all, and the top floor consisted only of an expensive restaurant one would have to patronize to piss in the pots of.

I climbed down the fire escape and figured I'd just go in the alley, but the alley below was actually a bazaar. I found the main street, entered the subway, and thought that perhaps a dark corner of the subway would suffice. My bladder was near bursting, and the story of Tycho Brahe's explosion began to ring in my memory.

However, the train arrived as soon as I reached the platform, and I was bustled inside. I made my way to the last car and looked longingly on the track behind us, but another train was directly on our heels.

I walked home from the station and thought about ducking into neighbors' back yards, but thoughts of arrest prevented me from going there.

By the time I got home, my teeth were floating. I rushed upstairs to the bathroom, but Lotte had locked herself in and was taking a bath. I went to the kitchen to use the sink, but Jackson and Alain were playing checkers at the table.

Finally, I hit upon a solution. I climbed into my bedroom closet, over the shoes, opened the window, pulled a chair in, stood on it, and pissed onto the rosebushes below. Never had a piss felt so good.

I had to go live by myself when I quit the university. Unfortunately, the only places I had keys for other than home were my car and my university offices and facilities.

One office was hidden on the fourth floor of a three-story building. At the top of the least-used emergency stairwell there was a forgotten storage area, formerly housing the building's air-conditioning units, which had been unused since all the campus air became synthesized centrally. Forgotten except by me. I had transfigured it.

Other than my living situation, I was free. I'd never let anyone like Edwin the Kleptomaniac impinge on my generosity again. Do someone a favor, and in turn he comes on to your wife and leaves his scuz in the tub for the kids to see. What would you do? Out the door immediately is the only way.

And then the stuff that was stolen: the Kiel Sailing Olympics brass bottle opener, back issues of *CLE* magazine, and a stuffed Tasmanian Devil doll—a "Taz." And other stuff, too.

I didn't like Edwin's being around anymore. He's bade farewell.

He's unwelcome even here, in this book.

The Unwelcome Guest

When I felt sure they were only a day away, I packed up and left. I figured I'd sleep in the car, but my plates had expired. I'd ordered and paid for them two months earlier but had not heard back, so I went to the tag office.

I told them I wanted to pick up my plates.

"No problem. That'll be $220."

"What? I already paid that."

"Not according to our records. If you want your plates, you have to pay $220."

"Oh, jeez. Another example of corruption in Georgia," I said.

"Then go back where you came from," said some fat white woman.

"Who are you?" I asked.

"The County Tax Commissioner."

"I'm offended by that. I'm a native Georgian, born in Atlanta in Crawford Long Hospital on Peachtree Street. I probably have more of a right to be here than you do." I left in disgust.

I went to the County Supervisor's office next door to complain but was intercepted by two policemen who said the tax commissioner had called and said I was drunk and threatening her. The police gave me a breathalyzer, saw my level was quite low, and told me to go home and cool off. I could come back tomorrow.

"They're just mad at me because I know too much," I told the police. "Like that $175,000 fire engine that can't be used." The city had bought the fire engine from "a friend." The engine had the Jaws of Life, which could pry open vehicles involved in major wrecks, as on the highway.

Unfortunately, the municipal fire department was not authorized to perform rescues on the highway, so the engine was used as a storage shed for Homeland Security equipment.

When I first moved to Macon, into an unfinished apartment, my wife saw the landlord giving the plumbing inspector $600. Immediately, without any more work done on it, the apartment building passed inspection.

I'll go, all right. I'll leave behind students who believe that Nelson Mandela was the first African-American to be elected president of South Africa, and that Christianity is a Father-Son relationship.

I'll gladly leave Georgia. But don't tell me where to go. No law requires I go home—I'll go where I please, thank you.

I'll visit my friend Anselm, a photographer who used to teach in Illinois. He'll sympathize with me now that I've stepped out of the system.

"There you go again, fool." He's called me that ever since we were classmates in high school. "Don't you know you can only effect change from within the system? That's why I've never stepped out of it. If you hadn't been afraid of the water in the first place..."

He was referring to the fact that I spent ten years out of school working in retail management before I decided to finish my degree and enter the professional world of academe.

I wondered then why I'd gone to visit him. He and his other friends, I suddenly remembered, had always had a habit of making themselves feel better in comparison by insulting anyone unlike themselves. Their derision of me—one idiot even suggested that for me writing wasn't an end in itself but merely a means to an end (what end? poverty? isolation? depression? What a fucking idiot!)—was plainly little more than the by-product of their own insecurities and narcissism.

Anselm was the only one of that bunch I respected, for he actually did his work. His triptychs were masterful examples of abstract narrative photography.

The other clowns? One joined the navy—I think he liked being rear-admiraled. He was the idiot who derided me about ends. Interesting. The other's a fat loud-mouthed piano instructor teaching little kids their Brimhall and Guy Duckworth. I'm sure he steers clear of the Bartok *Mikrokosmos*. Fats Loudmouth put out an album of modern classical music featuring Steerhorn 25 years earlier. It was an excellent and innovative piece of work, but he apparently had nothing else to say beyond that.

The three of them—Fats, Butt Boy, and Anselm, Anselm the least of them—had rolled their eyes at each other over my writing. Their monologues at me invariably began, "You know what your problem is?" or "You know why no one'll ever read your novels?" or "You wanna know what's wrong with your writing?"

They were all about talk... If the allegation is true that only two types of artist exist—artists who are busy doing their work and artists who are too busy "being artists," Fats and Butt Boy were the latter. Anselm was the former, but an observer would be hard-pressed to think so if watching Anselm around Fats and Butt Boy. Anselm would adapt, like a chameleon, to his environment, and in a crowd of loud-mouthed blowhards, he could keep his own and do a convincing impersonation of an artist too busy "being an artist."

His advice wasn't very helpful just then, but despite his pile-on tendencies in the company of thugs who were incapable of construction and who thus only committed destruction, I liked him. One-to-one Anselm could be a profoundly likeable observer of the world around him. Only this particular visit, though, he chose not to be.

So I made an excuse and left. Onwards to California! I barely made it to Chattanooga—the Georgia Mountains test my weariness—but with several emergency-caffeine rest stops, I made it. I just had to be out of Georgia before I could stop. The manhunters there couldn't follow me across state lines. They could stand there drooling of stupidity until their faces needed shaving—just long enough for me to make my getaway.

No—I lost them. Where to? Up to Illinois to see Anselm.

Anselm answered the door in a smoking jacket and silk slippers. He was gracious, but a bit aloof. He was perhaps as surprised as Fats and Butt Boy undoubtedly must have been that I'd achieved some modicum of success with my work. No doubt they believe I don't deserve it. I quickly felt uncomfortable and made my excuses.

Back on the road I couldn't get caught up in human foibles and soap opera relationships. "Hello" was superfluous when not followed by "good bye," and here one had no time for "good bye." The road-weary are a sullen, quiet group. If one encounters someone who is exuberant, that someone invariably turns out to be a local.

The exuberance of the driver is private, reserved as spare energy when all other energy is exhausted. Exuberance burns fast, though, and is normally one of the first energy sources to burn out. Ask any trucker.

I remember one time I was driving my rig—a full 18-wheeler. I had to tank up at this gas station I knew of at the intersection of two alleys in the warehouse district. I'd been drinking, so I wasn't at my best, and I pulled up short at the pump—the nozzle reached to a foot away from my gas cap. I had to get back in the cab and pull forward some more, which was a little embarrassing. I pushed past a couple of smoking busybodies by the pump. Right as I was about to reach for the cap to open it again, the rig started moving. Oh, shit, I thought. I'd forgotten to apply the brake. The rig rolled ahead and then made a sharp turn, barely missing the building across the alley. It swung around and then barreled into one of the warehouses. I heard an explosion and figured I was in serious trouble. I was facing negligence and DUI, for sure. The owner of the gas station, though, was a friend—a gray-haired fatherly fellow. He called the police and told them someone had stolen the rig from the pump and had smashed it during the getaway. I figured he was being nice to cover for me like that. I excused myself and went to the bathroom, which was an enormous locker room. My pants were soaked with beer from my open can that had spilled on me during the drive. I figured if I didn't get out of those pants, I'd be arrested. I pulled my shirttails down as far as they'd go and hoped for the best. I shoved my pants into a locker. When the police came, the officer, the owner and I stood together to discuss what had happened. When the officer looked down at her pad, the owner, under the guise of straightening my glasses, slipped a palmed breath mint into my mouth. I figured I must reek of booze. The officer and the owner seemed to be friends, though, so when the owner explained the truck-jacking, the officer told him that it probably had something to do with the disturbance at the parade over the weekend—that this had been orchestrated by the same people who'd orchestrated that disturbance. What disturbance or what parade I had no idea, but the two of them sure did. The owner nodded in agreement. After the officer had taken our statements, I walked to the elevated train. The officer followed me. She sat opposite me and started talking about how she had to ride the train to and from the police station because her car had been wrecked during the parade riots.

I got off the train at Central, the next-to-last stop. The officer must have been continuing on to Linden, the end station. I went into the station bathroom—also a locker room—and on a hunch opened a locker and found a pair of pants that fit. The station contained a coffee shop, which was run by a young 20-something couple who were very much in love. I had some coffee and shot the breeze with them, teasing them a little for their young love.

I left the coffee shop and stood outside by the bus stop. No bus was in sight. I realized I'd left my cigarettes and my Arno Schmidt book that I always carried with me in the coffee shop. I went back in and for the first time noticed a display of t-shirts for sale inside the station. The shirts were a motley collection of sports teams, rock bands, and glib sayings. I went back into the coffee shop, commented sarcastically on the t-shirts, and picked up my cigarettes and book. The coffee shop guy tried to crack a joke about Schmidt, but it wasn't funny. I left.

Outside I saw an old man had come to wait for the bus as well. Then I realized that in my offense I'd forgotten my book and cigarettes again. I went back to the coffee shop again and picked up the Schmidt book but couldn't see the cigarettes. I'd assumed the coffee shop guy had taken them, but before I accused him, I checked my pockets and found I had them in my shirt breast pocket.

Outside again, the old man and I talked about weather and the disintegration of the moral fiber of our nation. The bus came. Once seated aboard, I fell asleep.

The old man shook me awake. He told me we'd come to the next-to-last stop and that he had to get off. He told me he lived in a building down an alley a few blocks away. I was unfamiliar with it, but he said the people who lived there always complained. The owner was a slumlord, he said. He left. The next stop was mine, so there I got off.

Now I remember what the police officer had told me: they suspected that the man behind the parade bombings was one Edwin L. Thoth. Small world.

I, years earlier, had written a small volume on Thoth. I had written it in a pre-bound blank book and had intended to photocopy it for someone. I tried to tear the pages out of the book, but accidentally tore an enormous chunk out of the center of that group of pages. The chunk fell, flaked apart, and flew away into the river, so much of the text of the piece disappeared. I was unable to reconstruct what the text had once been.

I remember the previous year's downtown parade. Christmas shopping season afflicted the city. I was working part-time in the largest multi-story bookstore in the city. We were fending for and fending off dozens of customers simultaneously, all of whom were demanding and labor-intensive. When my hour lunch break arrived, I went outside to meet a buddy, a co-worker whom I was going to have lunch with—or "drunch," as we called it. I couldn't find him in the crowd outside, so I walked down to the south Loop bar by myself. Or I was going to. I was stopped by a parade a block away between me and my destination. I could see the enormous balloons and papier-mâché constructs going by—skyscrapers the size of skyscrapers and busses the size of office buildings were moving along the street. I realized I'd never get to the bar and back with time left over for sufficient drinking, so I instead went to one of the more expensive bars on State Street. Fortunately, happy hour had hit, and the drinks came with all-you-can-eat hot wings. I don't remember ever going back to the store.

Maybe Edwin was there, selling balloons. He'd done that for a while, working for the over-inflated balloon lady. I have a photo of him somewhere, caught with dentures between flaps—he'd flap them around in his mouth—Snap! Dangle! Snap!—because he was too cheap to buy adhesive. He sold balloons until he slept with the balloon lady and her husband found out. You could say her husband popped that balloon. Her name was Armenia and her husband was a turkey. Neither of them gave Edwin a second thought. Until they disappeared underground. Literally. That was when I discovered that Edwin was a master of disguise and was also known by the name "Lubjec," which might be what the "L" stood for. "Lawrence" might have been a fabrication.

Cities

At 3:10, I intended to leave for a trip to the city. A church there had a position for an organist, and, well, the bank I was in wasn't making it. I'd had to play part-time at a mock-Christian bar, and I'd fake it so well some folks thought I could pass for the real thing. So they asked me to guest-play as one of three finalists for the job.

I was waiting for the bus with a box of jelly doughnuts on my lap when I remembered my dry cleaning. I ran to get it. I couldn't afford to miss the bus because the President would be speaking at noon.

I'd forgotten about the doughnuts, which smashed all over me in vibrant colors.

The dry cleaners had lost the top front button to my suit, a detail I did not notice until the most embarrassing possible moment later. But I did make the bus. For a few blocks.

Then the bus broke down. And I hadn't had time even to change my clothes.

"What's the big idea?" you may be thinking.

Precisely! No big idea. Build gradually. See how the building wants to be built.

I walked back to the bus stop. That had been the last bus for the day, she said. Then she laughed at my clothes.

"It's not funny," I said.

"It sure is!" she laughed.

"Ha ha," I said, and then I started laughing too. Then I stopped. "The bad thing is I'm going to have to miss the President's speech."

The Unwelcome Guest

"Nah. You can watch it on C-Span. Come on—my shift is over anyway." Out of the shadows stepped her replacement—a fifty-year-old Chinese man.

As we left, she asked me what I did for a living. I couldn't answer "church organist," so I told her the name of the band I'd been in.

"Hey," she said. "Do you mind my asking if you have a girlfriend?"

At that moment I knew she liked me.

We went to a bar, and she sang Matchbox Twenty while we shot some 9-ball. I knew then that I liked her, too.

We started dating. Oh, the best dating I've ever known. She was fun, intelligent, beautiful...all I could ask for in someone. She was fantastic!

And then she went away.

But she came back! So I won't dwell on going away. The coming back is so much more important.

It glows. Warming us, illuminating us. Our burdens have become light. We lift off and hang-glide alongside each other. We dip, falling into the water and rising back out into the sky again. We can fly through the mouths of volcanoes into the heart of magma, through the core and out the other side of the earth. We fly the spool between north and south poles.

We are bathed in aqua vitae.

She says we don't live in a democracy—we live in a representative republic.

She's right.

But most activists are hedge trimmers. Most real writers are root-killers.

Ah, off to Hasty Generalization land again, I see. You always go there.

"As do you."

"Nurse, he's talking to himself again."

"Okay—here. Give him this lozenge."

I try to unwrap it, but it's melted to the wrapper. I can't pull the lint off it. The lint's not even mine. I remember—it was the third Sunday before lint..."

"No! Don't do that! For once?"

"And the band played on..."

"Not at the price of clichés, it doesn't. Groundrules: no clichés, no fuzzy animals, no soap operas..."

"No whoppers, no tall tales..."

"No redundancy or repeating oneself."

"Nice sarcasm!"

"No invective, asshole!"

"No bombast, you pusillanimous fool!"

"Less negativity. Bummer."

"What? It can't be a tragedy? Then how will it ever be taken seriously?"

"Ah..."

And we agree. So we're asking you—an' you take the wheel for a while. I'm too out of it to keep driving. Thanks. It's been a long day.

How's your day been? Hopefully okay.

If not, well, hey—I understand.

The Unwelcome Guest

I'm actually doing well right now. I have an amazing fiancée. My writing and publishing are blossoming. My teaching is dying. There's the tragedy.

"I mean bigger."

Okay okay. It's a big deal to me. Sorry. So let me tell you this story.

Sure.

A fish was swimming in the sunstreams. He'd surface in the epicenter of splashes. He sewed the ocean shut.

The birds cried out, "Oh, tailors of fish, come to us so we might save our friends the fish from suffocation."

The tailors honored the request and opened the ocean. The birds began to dive and catch the fish. Coleridge betrayed the albatross.

If fifteen men ate eggs for breakfast, not one would have praised the albatross. Thanks to Coleridge. What was he? High?

Oh, yeah. I guess he was. Now *I* would never do anything like that, mind you.

Quiet, you back there. I'm trying to sink.

Better let it out, then.

We need more colors down here. We're tired of it always being blue.

That's the request?

Sure.

Cool. Thanks.

People need this stuff flung at them in big chunks. Just to awaken them.

Uh...

"Sorry. Just thinking out loud."

Happens to us all.

Not all. There you go again.

Sorry. I'll try to notice from now on. Old habits, eh?

Are like old houses? Yeah, I've heard that. No clichés!

Sorry, boss.

Cut it out.

Hey, what'd be cool is if we went somewhere.

Together.

Yeah, all of us [gesturing towards us].

Where'd you have in mind?

My upcoming marriage.

Congratulations, man.

Thanks. I'm lucky.

Beware of clichés!

Okay. She is ubiquitous in my future. Her presence will bless every day.

Time for a change?

Mr. President, anything except blue, please. We're way tired of yellow. Black and white invite race comparisons. Red is dead.

Green is ambiguous enough, perhaps.

So what do you say, Mr. President?

I once wrote a letter to the Mayor of Macon and another to the Superintendent of the Bibb County School Board. A friend of mine wrote the latter a letter as well. We never received replies. My conclusion is that these individuals must be illiterate. I see no evidence of any literary life. Those with no literary life are illiterate.

Of course, the President on TV did not respond to my question. My love didn't know why I kept talking to the TV.

The Unwelcome Guest

This was the question I'd saved up for him. Logic, compassion, entreaty, fair-mindedness had been proven beyond his abilities. I thought color might work. One of the President's friends (a televangelist, incredibly) never grew past purple. People get hung up on colors. Funny, eh?

A pure obelisk beckoned mauve magpies to drop aquamarine presents onto it. I walk past it every day on the way to work. What do I do? I edit a magazine; *Your Expansive Future*. Don't ask. It's a living. I'll tell you about it later.

My advice: when people tell you how to write, smile and nod and then let your eyes glaze over, yawn, and turn to talk to someone interesting.

She calls me from the kitchen: "Can I get you anything?"

"A beer would be nice," I reply.

"All I have is Pajama Brew."

"It'll do. Thanks." Fermented pajama squeezin's. Oh well. If it's cold enough. "Is it cold?"

"Ice cold."

"Perfect. Thanks."

"Want it on ice?"

"No, no. You don't do that with beer."

"Really? I do."

"Well, you're an oddball. That's probably why I love you."

"Really? I love you too, for many reasons. Metaphysical and emotional."

"And physical?"

"Of course. You know that."

"I suppose I do."

I'm at her house right now. It's 2:30, and I have to be in at 9:00. I can't sleep, though. We were in the middle of making love when her nine-year-old son walked in. He was sleepy, but it freaked her out. We didn't get back to making love, so I'm sitting here writing. I love her.

Turn off the soap opera. I hear you. But you know, life does actually contain soap opera moments and corny moments and why not include them? To not do so is to oversimplify life.

But still, you'd probably like a story to pin this on. Onward, Charles! Remember—to be fashionable means you can be fashioned into things. We pathetic humans never seem to forget having been fashioned. Now we are as mere ceramic playthings. Make sure you get good and glazed before you get fired.

I leave her place and walk home. The obelisk is lit. In the night haze, it takes on a bluish aura. The aura moves, like oscilloscope lines, in the rhythms of my *muscae volitantes*.

The fog-dampened boardwalk on the edge of the sea is nearly empty—a few persistent anglers still cast from the pier; a small family walks barefoot by the water's edge; a dead brown pelican lies in a heap at the end of the pier, next to the garbage can. The garbage can is filled with dead pelicans.

The cemetery nearby is filled with dead anglers. Death has been busy this year. He deserves a year off. At least. Several boards on the walk need replacing. The risks of falling through and being seriously injured are great. Even so—I was taught to skip by an old sea captain Irish mountain goat.

At the end of the boardwalk is the entrance to a path into the woods that stretch for dozens of miles in any direction except binary. The true stars are they who deny the opposition total supremacy. Or so De Saussure might have said. Who's to know? Gigi or G.G. Allen? Is it all a matter of taste? Or is that a false dichotomy?

Quick—the door! Out here! Quick!

I follow him. He slams the door.

"Oh, man. I couldn't take one more second of that." he says.

"Me, either," I confess. He leads me into a hidden tavern underneath the boardwalk.

"If you're headin' into those woods, you're gonna need some bolstering," says he.

Instead, I go into the city. I find a bar made of soap. Convenient should I pass out on my stool, slide my face across the bar and wake up ready for a shave. I could use a laser, the newest way to shave out of the East.

Yeah, smart ass, why don't you Kanji then.

Sorry—I didn't mean anything.

That's just it. You never mean anything.

Oh, well *that's* nice.

Hush! Do you see that?

The entrance to the woods. Do I have to?

He nods.

I'm in. The trees are weak here on the outskirts. Lots of bare limbs.

Hey, get your mind out of the gutter! He yells.

I'm referring to the trees, I yell back.

I see Jim Chapman coming back the other way.

"How're the woods?" I ask.

"Freaky. I just wrote about them."

"Oh." Better find some new ground.

This time make sure it hasn't already been taken.

Gerdes and Chapman, in a land grab for material, race neck and neck.

Actually, it's not like that. Material shared is material urned. So, of course, I razed the forest and retreated into the city where nothing is natural.

Nothing in my life is natural.

I am an artificial man, at least on a cellular level. Re-entering the city, I see the design patterns made by the lit lights of the high-rise buildings lining streets like chess pieces. In this game, though, all are pawns.

Wake up! Your country brethren aren't going to help! The Kraken has swallowed all your lovers' lovin', so there ain't none left for you.

Nor will there ever be. Love died with the computer commuter for whom sex is just another plug-in. You hear me? You! Over there on the seat riding sideways! How many cities can one heart hold? Mine holds Atlanta, Kiel, Geneva, Mulungwishi, Cape Town, Nashville, Chicago, Iowa City, Dubuque, Anchorage, and Macon, all for having lived there. Add to that list of cities I've slept in and you'll see there is in my heart precious little space. Any one city is big enough to fill the space.

Unable to leave the city, I decide to find my way down-town. I buy a Bosc pear at a kiosk and a newspaper out of a machine. I find a seat on a bench in the park. The Staples Singers are playing a gospel festival.

What? In the city?

Certainly. It's Gospelfest or something.

Is Mahalia there?

No, man, she passed a while ago.

As I weave my way towards the stage, I see my shoe-lace has come undone. I bend down to tie it and some bozo galumphs into me from behind. I go rolling like a bowling ball into a group of furniture sales representatives out for a Sunday stroll.

"No," says one, "I always argue that the loveseat is an essential part of any living room. That way you have seats to accommodate groups of one, two *or* three."

"Is one a group?"

"Well...you know—I *do* have schizoid friends."

"Ah..."

"And people who are satisfied by themselves."

"Oh!"

"And a mosquito bite on the back of my knee that's driving me insane. Please excuse me." He takes off and goes into the can.

Another takes his place. "He's a crackpot," says she. "Any couple in a loveseat would rather be in the bedroom," says she. "That much is obvious."

The city talks thus. The country is subtler.

Driving home, I hear the debate. I try to make it home, but I fall asleep and crash on the way—

"I can't wait."

The grid engulfs me. My fingers and toes become enmeshed in it. Then the ground gives way. The city spires jut up at me, spearing me in the side. The churches have no idea what they've done, spearing the heavens.

The city is a confidence artist. No, not artist. The city hates the artist. The city is an assembly-line worker. What's being manufactured are the citizens. I believe I am my social security number, my driver's license number, my phone number.

This is no mere village.

Some things add just a fine eloquence.

Something's adjusting vanilla quince.

Don't you?

My nails are pulled from my fingers and toes. They are replaced by hatred, with hate, from the hateful.

And the north seems to beckon. Leave the city: go to the inhospitable zone, it suggests. But I see through that trick. If I crawl off to die in the woods, the city won't have to deal with me. Well, me they're going to find skewered on their main spire. Unless I succeed in shutting it down, which I don't want to do. A shut down city is the scariest thing in the world.

I've seen fifteen cities shut down in the last thirty years—rioting, looting, excessive force, casualties—these are the results.

Waving back and forth in the breeze, the rhythm is ambient reggae. I'd say it was romantic, but I've been told I have no idea what romance is, so it must be something different. Ask my wives—they know how romantic I am. Ask the second especially. The first didn't really like me much. Oh, that's not true. She just tired of me quickly. It's not easy living with me. For one thing, I do not like filling out forms.

Remember: you only have the right to assembly if you fill out the proper forms. You only have the right to free speech if you fill out the proper forms.

I remember one man, Lubjec, I think his name was, who couldn't fill out forms either. He was a neighbor of mine in an apartment building in Old Town. He told me he so agonized over filling out forms, he'd gotten sick, so his job fired him. After that he just stayed home and filled out every form he could find. I do not want to become him.

Of course, he didn't have a car like mine: a charcoal 2000 Toyota Camry. What a car—the best sled I ever had —or does "sled" only refer to motorcycles? I forget.

Nor did he have my wife. Well, she's not really my wife, legally, but in every other sense she is. Know what I mean? And—I don't mind bragging—she is amazing.

The President on TV asks, "Are you willing to make sacrifices for your country?" I imagine huge Viking pyres consuming domestic artists, but I guess he meant on a personal level, and, no—I will not sacrifice my wife for anything or anyone. I then notice the President is wearing a dark green suit. Excellent. The last one wouldn't wear green. The Mayor had condemned him for it, which was awkward during the convention because the Mayor, of course, was a delegate in his home city, which hosted the convention. Lubjec of all people, ended up kidnapping the Mayor. Of course, the police, once they found him, shot him in self-defense while he slept. The Mayor, having been rescued, had ordered the shooting. And then all of Lubjec's neighbors had to be questioned, of course. Wonderful. The Mayor's secret police didn't take long to find where I was, and I only barely escaped—my downstairs neighbor tipped me off when they came to her door. She called me and left the phone off the hook so I could hear everything. I was gone before the second sentence. No way was I going back to jail.

I moved to another city where, as I said, I became a church organist in a rock band.

No wonder a small place like Grand Rapids had had some appeal to me, though I knew I couldn't be there long in the land of the thumped. I'd like to say we got there without a hitch, but my wife got very sick—I think from the morphine inhalant tubes we'd been drinking. I had to get her off the bus long before we made it to the city. I can't remember where exactly it was—we were pretty high— but it was a big city. I remember seeing a bar open from seven am to seven pm.

I remember jeeps rolling though the streets. It was a city under martial law, I think. How we escaped the city I don't recall. My wife might know. But probably not. We woke up two days later back in our city and we weren't sure if we'd actually gone on a trip until I found the gas receipts. I'm not sure who signed for half of them—the handwriting's neither mine nor hers, but it resembles Lubjec's, strangely. But that couldn't be. He was dead. Or so the police had told us. Who knows if they are telling the truth, though. Frequently they don't.

The Unwelcome Guest

The President has formed a commission to look into reported abuses by big city cops. I'm sure the commission will never be heard of again—it was a salve announcement.

It's a Salve New World, Little People. Do as you're told and you won't get hurt. I think that's the gist of his message.

Of course, we freaked out when we came to. I mean, there we were, hunted for questioning, and we returned to our lair. We got out of there fast, amazed that the police hadn't staked our place out, or had they? Had our return been at their hands? Were we being watched? We weren't sure. How could we be? When I caught her looking at me suspiciously, I knew we had to move again. That would keep her distracted. We moved six times in four months, until she trusted me again. By then, we'd picked up six species of cockroach in our boxes. We finally decided to fumigate. We set off our bombs and went to a motel. When we got back the next day, our apartment had been ransacked. They had found us again.

You can imagine this wasn't easy on my wife's nerves. She Who Has Thus Far Been Unnamed needs a name. She's not Beckett's—she's mine. Her name is Suzette.

Ah! So you say that she and Beckett were both French? No! Beckett was as Irish as James Joyce. Ireland always pushes her young away from her bosom. In this, she and America are sisters. America only lets multi-national oil conglomerates suck on her tits. Blessed are the French, who accept us from peasant stock!

A French woman, out of some incredible generosity, took us in. We stayed in her house and were given a room with southern exposure. Suzette loved it, and brought dozens of plants: green, white, red, gold, blue.

How we met her is interesting. I was carrying a book by Raymond Federman, *Aunt Rachel's Fur*, around, and this woman at this restaurant came over and told us she's read it—in French, of course—and that she thought it the funniest, most ribald writing since Rabelais. We hit it off. Suzette seemed a little jealous, but when Suzette—yes, they had the same name—invited us to coffee, my Suzette immediately accepted, which allayed my fears. I love my Suzette. I would never betray her. The Suzettes became good friends, actually. They played tennis together at least three times a week.

I kept myself busy by reading avant-garde fiction—you really should read it if you haven't. Oh, you have been?

And now, five am, after a night of writing, my demons confront me. Not with any ferocity. See? City is at the heart of many things.

For two months I had no idea that the other Suzette had known Lubjec. Lubjec had, apparently, survived and had gone underground. Literally. Supposedly he'd built himself an underground city, a project he'd been working on for twenty years. As the underground city grew, it dug deeper, because it knew the surface would crash down eventually.

Each underground city was built under a big city. When the top worlds collapsed, the lower worlds would dominate. Like icebergs, big cities showed only ten percent of their mass above surface. Then they collapsed. The lower worlders were already too deep to be affected. The upper worlders died. Most of them. A few of us made it. And we formed a resistance.

I'm their unwilling scribe, Jacobus.

Excuse me—the President's back on. The power outages in the city are no cause for concern, he says. The city police, as always, have everything completely under control.

Control.

What a word. Buck Henry and Mel Brooks, in *Get Smart*, seem to have thought the word positive: Control were the good guys, CHAOS the bad. Others might posit "freedom" as positive, "control" as negative. What do you make of that?

Staying at Suzette's (Suzette H., not my wife, Suzette M.) was a delightful respite from the world's woes. That's what I'm supposed to say. The truth is, that it was hell. My wife's jealousy got worse. She began to imagine I was referring to the other Suzette when I called out her name in bed. It was crazy. I only think about *my* Suzette. Her face. Her smile. Her freckles. Her dimples. The curve of her mouth. The expression in her eyebrow. Her deep brown, almost black, eyes that are the abyss that can engulf a man forever. Now do you see how much I love her? My Suzette, I mean.

I must pause here.

I must panic here. The philosophy of the city: "I'm no longer myself. I'm exactly who you want."

I have been assigned to find Lubjec. I de-atomize tonight.

The process is simple. Each of my atoms will be programmed to find him. When one locates him, the rest receive the message and reassemble before him.

That should freak him out. Hopefully that alone will be enough to make him surrender.

My atoms speed into the entryway to the underground, then they disperse. They zoom down corridors.

"Halt! You can't go in there," led to I did. A few air conditioning vents later, I found him. I was behind him, so I started toward him.

He was wearing a baseball uniform. His name was sewn onto the back. I saw a team name, the Hawkinsville Homers, so I dispersed and rethought my strategy before he saw me.

I wondered what he was doing in the city. On a hunch, I bought a paper. Sure enough, the Homers were in town to play the city's minor league team. Lubjec was listed as P.J. Ribl, but I read anagrams. I recognized him.

Why take him so fast? I wondered. I could jinx his game, have some fun.

Great Googlymoogly! There. That ought to fix him. Now to take a seat in the stands. "Ladies and Gentlemen! Welcome to William Weaver Field!"

Oh, good. The starting line-ups. Excellent! Ribl was starting at second. That was a little odd, because he was normally the shortstop. But the regular second baseman, Legron, was nowhere to be seen, and the game had to be played on time. One thing for sure, Skipper Leo "Minnie" Dumocher wouldn't have gone easy on Legron even if he had been killed in a car accident.

The Unwelcome Guest

Oh, look at that. On a hit-and-run fly to left, on an attempt to double-up the base runner, who was already past second, Ribl had tried to back up first base. However, the pitcher had the same idea. Ribl and the pitcher collided on the other side of the first baseman, and Ribl's staying down. The pitcher seems to be okay. He'd hit his head into Ribl's temple. Ribl's out. Man, a concussion at least. I hope he's okay. Oh—better get up and go to the concession stand now. There'll be a long wait in a few minutes. Plus there'll be too many people in the men's room for me to get into a stall, and I hate competition urination. Oh, that's right. The stalls here don't even have doors. I hate public defecation, also. I see little to be gained by humiliating the fans, but then that's me. Others seem to get off on it.

However, there are those who try to get off on humiliating me. One favorite play is to insult me. Another is to insult my children. Any insult leveled at my children is leveled at me. My advice is not to go there.

Of course, no one listens to me. A favorite sport of those whom I know is to pretend they care about me, but when the crunch is on, to deny any knowledge of me. Before my cock crows twice, they've condemned me. Of course.

Not *my* cock of course. Mine crows a hundred thirty or forty times at least before I'm condemned. There's no rule, naturally, that says women should hate their men. There are very few rules, actually.

I've made it too easy to hate me, haven't I? I'd better go read some Arno Schmidt again. It's all about the sentences we're given.

Life. Eternity with someone who hates you. Sartre's *No Exit*. That's all right. If it's a test, I'll pass. Even when hated, I am faithful. It is the one quality consistent in me. I never betray my mate.

She, of course, despises me for it, wishing I were unfaithful so her hatred would be justified.

Her hatred of me is eye-opening! I've been used. Ah, well, my ship is back for me soon.

On board will be provisions for my feelings as well as my hunger and thirst. Stowaways might tell me I'm a good captain—my first mate apparently finds doing so demeaning. However, I still trust my first mate and will not find in the stowaways a replacement. As I said, I am loyal, even if no one else is. I'll stay here and work crosswords. I'm safe in my cabin.

A knock.

I ignore it.

Another.

I ignore it, too. I have work to do. I'm not looking for love again. It becomes hate. I don't understand the rules of trinkets, phone calls, ex-husbands, or whatever is in that jewelry box. I can announce a tornado by accident—I savvy the weather. I know when to duck. It's duck season. I have my waders on. I crouch. Low-flying projectiles are heading at me. I'm being told again that I'm the sorriest human who has ever lived. It's okay—I've been hated before. I don't think it's permanent.

Mark her. She's got the ball now. Intercept it when she tries to pass.

The Unwelcome Guest

Scootch in between the smooch? Sorry—we may be having problems, but we're still together. You'd better keep away, or your fingers will get burned, even on the moon. Get in the way, I'll push you aside. Sorry. I'm okay now. All is well in paradise.

Other pressing issues abound.

The fish tank is filled with shrimp. One fish is jealous of them. The other systematically spits them out of the tank. The apartment is hot. The box fans are no better than the oscillating ones. A/C? Don't make me laugh. In those days I was lucky to have shoes.

When I walk barefoot through the apartment, shrimp squish between my toes. The smell is a little strong, but I just smoked more to cover it and went about my business as if nothing were wrong. I figured I could psych out the fish this way so that they'd stop spitting. That didn't work.

I'm losing tenseness.

No one really believes this is happening now, does hir?

We're afraid to go outside. Strangers are out there. They could fuck us over. So we figure out how to fuck 'em over first.

Put 'em on a starship blaster space, flang 'em toward the straysystem out alone on the edge of time: blast 'em through onto an exploding A. They grab at the cross-bar. Hold on. Implosion follows explosion. Come back out looking at the poster on the wall.

Yeah, I remember all that. City-dwelling at its alonest. Very educational, though.

Oh, the B is 'bout to go. Hold on. Oh, well. Still 24 left. The knocking on my door is getting to me. C just went.

Now D. Everything's still fine. From now it's not. Go E. Go F. Go G. How will I try to...

III. Something New

She's sleeping next to me in bed. She's going to wake up worrying that she disappointed me by just going to sleep. She hasn't. Just being next to her is a privilege.

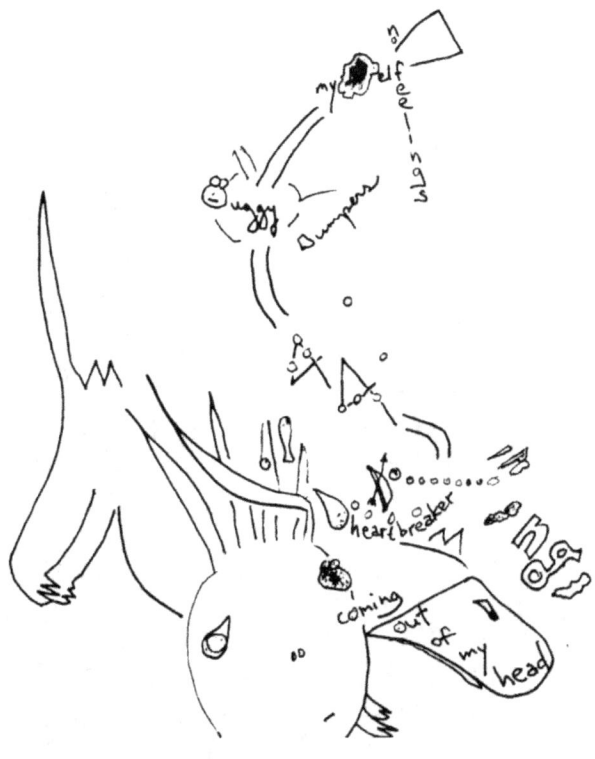

I'll be your reptile tonight
while we freeze the food.
I'm not dressing for the fashion show.

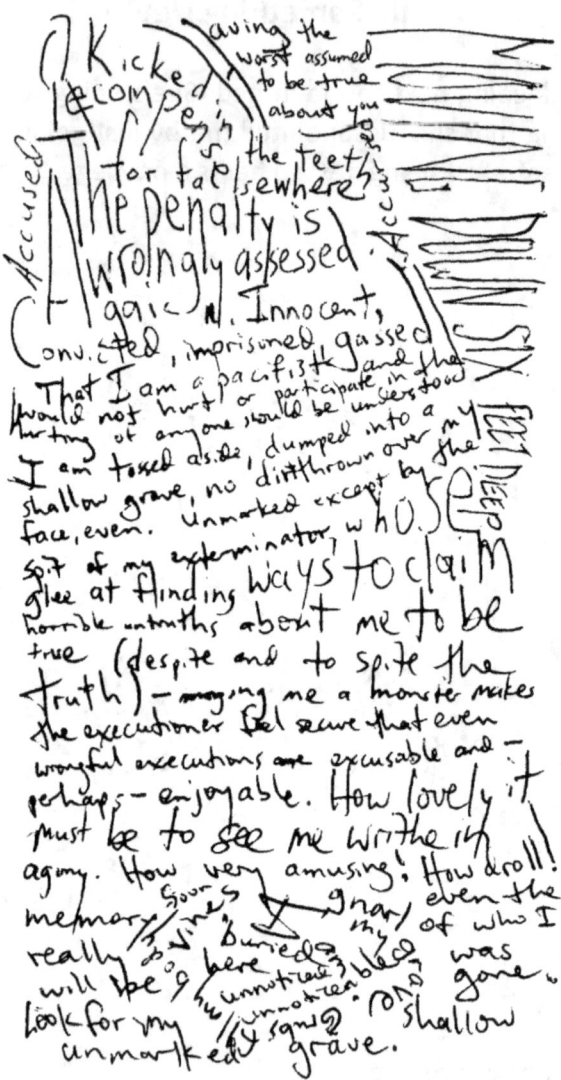

Kicked

aving the worst assumed to be true about you

competin'

for far sewhere?

the teeth

Accused

The penalty is wrongly assessed.

Tragic. Innocent, convicted, imprisoned, gassed

That I am a pacifist and that would not hurt or participate in the hurting of anyone should be understood I am tossed aside, dumped into a shallow grave, no dirt thrown over my face, even. Unmarked except by the spit of my exterminator, whose glee at finding ways to claim horrible untruths about me to be true (despite and to spite the truth) — making me a monster makes the executioner feel secure that even wrongful executions are excusable and — perhaps — enjoyable. How lovely it must be to see me writhe in agony. How very amusing! How droll! memory gnaw even the of who I really buried was gone. Look for my shallow unmarked grave.

MOVING DOWN SIX FEET DEEP

The Unwelcome Guest

The red queen points at me
and yells, "Off with his head!"
Decapitated, I have only moments
to defend myself against lies,
before my body collapses
on the killing floor and spasms.
I voice the word, "I,"
and realize I sound pathetic,
selfish, solipsistic, narcissistic.
"Am" next, sounding Cartesian,
pseudointellectual, unemotional,
cold, uncaring, doubting.
I could stop there, but I
continue into futility, breathing
a final tri-syllabic death-rattle:
"innocent." By then, all have gone.
No one hears the last word.

I can't move. I'm in Earth-sha. This telepathic message will be years old before you hear it. Do not respond. I will be gone. I need to warn you. You are in danger. Don't look behind yourself. You don't have time. Here—this way. Maybe I can help this way. But whatever you do, don't come looking for me. You will not be welcomed. Just listen. I'm no threat. I can't move. I am not asking for help. I am not asking you to cure my immobility. My immobility is necessary. Forget about me, but hear me out. You also have the mark of being in Earth-sha. You are being sedentary right now.

MAP OF IN-EARTH-SHA

A watched pot never grows. It's paint-by-numbers in book form: conventional fiction. Vines are lazy plants.

Touchdown. Extra point. Kick off. Fumble. Touchdown. Extra point. Kick off. Fumble. That's the way to win 222-0.

The Unwelcome Guest

The dog's off chasing rabbits. Its barking awakens her.

The furniture goes in the garbage. The bag of garbage goes in the truck: I still have to sort through that garbage.

Orange juice without breakfast is like sunshine without a day. Marketeers ripped our flesh. Yeah—we'll share time with you in hell before we buy your time share. Model airplanes were kamikaziing into alligators. Salesmen using submission holds on the elderly and on foreigners; charlatans whipping children with the children's own eyebrows; sexist suits making jokes about menses and Mensa: you should be ashamed of the predatory nature of your occupation!

We withstood the attack. Blackened grouper helped. We held each other.

Now, she is sleeping next to me in bed. Beautiful, peaceful. I wish for her an easy day tomorrow.

We are in our state room cabin now. I hear her breathing as I write. I think that her breaths are mine also. Without her breath, I could not breathe. Without her smile, I have no interest in smiling. Without her touch, nothing touches me.

Seven-foot swells keep me on my back for some two or three hours. Nausea threatens my filet mignon dinner and my rum punch happy hour cocktails. This ship holds thousands of twisted tourists—I would never have thought it small enough to be batted about so easily by waves and wind.

This is the worst nausea I've felt since before my marriage. A long time ago, I darted a fertilizer saleswoman. If ever a profession was a metaphor for a life, hers was.

The nausea was as bad as that disgust I felt at the Peanut-Brained Writing Awards Ceremony, where the category winners comprised former judges, employees and even chefs working inside the organization—the most obvious award-fixing since Charles You-Know-Who's resignation from the National Book Award committee was rewarded with the award itself. Or the university writing department that groomed student stories for the state's largest daily newspaper's annual creative writing contest, which was "coincidentally" judged by the same faculty. What a surprise that only that university's students ever won the awards. The general public had no chance. Thus in my writing the via college gave way to the via collage.

The nausea reminded me of sitting in the back seat of my parents' station wagon as my father sped along twisted mountain roads when we visited our vacation home, an A-frame near Gatlinburg, Tennessee. Blackie, our German shepherd, locked in a cage in the back, lying atop a pile of old burlap potato sacks, competed with me to see who would hurl first.

Javelins fly over bridges; shots are put into arms; discs are slipped through bars; pies are chipped onto farms.

In Earth-sha we all smoke. It drains our energy so that we sit still and notice before acting. Of course, normally we fall asleep before we do anything. Smoking is isolating: the individual can maintain her or his distance by putting up a wall of smoke. Of course, even where you are, one could find people holding smoking up as a defense against normalization. The more it is outlawed, the greater its appeal. That is why the tobacco companies are funding the anti-tobacco advertising. It's like that here, too.

Let's put our differences aside for the Olympics.

The Mexicans won the jumping bean contest. The Peruvians fared poorly. Or course, they were using Lima beans.

I can't wait to see the swimmers submerged in Greece.

The Central Asian middleweight boxers were impressive. Uzbekhistan, Azerbaijan and Kazakhstan were represented well.

I had pork chops for dinner. Martina Navratilova is playing doubles for the US versus the Ukraine. That's lady's an amazing tennis player. A southpaw. The court has "windy conditions"? It looks indoor, but can't be.

The world is becoming uncultured, but that's what it wants—not for the Olympics, but for the lack of equal celebration for the arts down to equal subcategories equivalent to synchronized diving. Experimental fiction would contain dozens of subcategories. Ah, pipe dreams, as O'Neill would say.

Our world is aggressively shedding its mantel of art. Or is America alone in this as well? Should it hang its head and look aside while its artists are silenced? The marketplace silences them. Commodification silences them. Competition silences them.

We're not writing for baubles or trinkets, are we? Respectability means something. No?

We're not a carny sideshow of solipsists on ice. And we're not all heathens.

We're civilized and shovelized and randomized until the order looks like chaos.

We're winterized and Simonized and Martinized until we're purple.

We're Dewey-decimated, baseball-captivated, digitally calibrated poor s.o.b.'s who despise forming plurals with apostrophes.

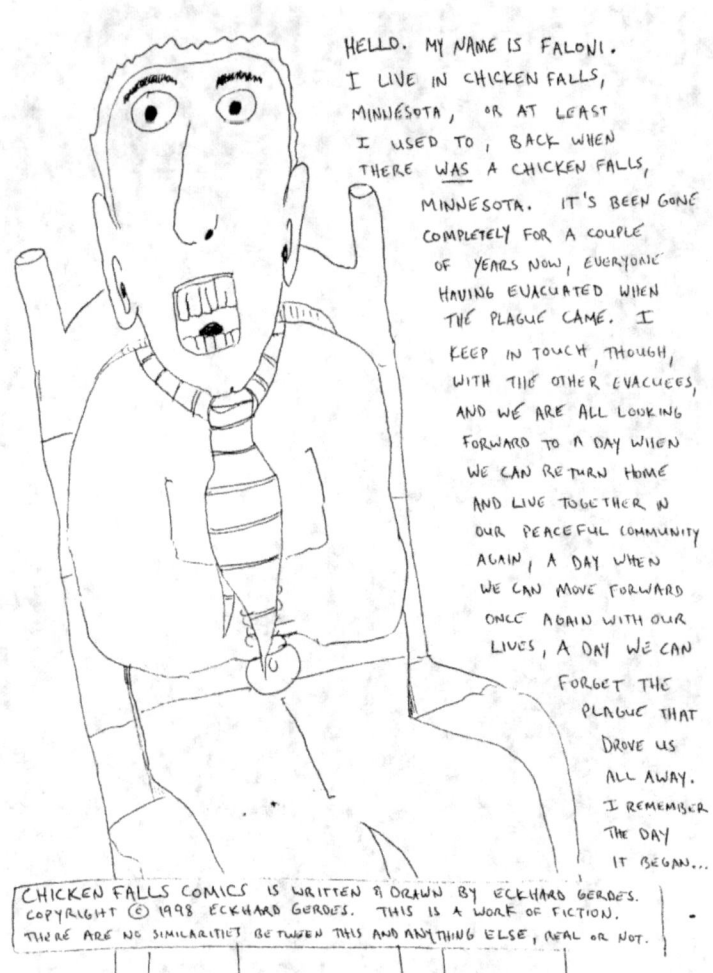

The Unwelcome Guest

IT WAS TEA-TIME IN THE MIRROR STORE ...

OWNED BY A VERY STRANGE OLD WOMAN WHO LOOKED AT ME LIKE SHE WAS CLEOPATRA AND I WAS HER HEADDRESS

BUT ACTUALLY THE ONLY HEADPIECE SHE EVER WORE WAS HER BIRD MASK, TO FEND OFF PLAGUE.

OVER SCONES SHE'D WARN US ABOUT THE CHICKENS, AND THE PLAGUE THEY'D BRING DOWN ON US. WE ALWAYS FIGURED HER TO BE SOME CRAZY OLD LADY WHO MADE GREAT TEA AND PASTRY, BUT WE EVENTUALLY FOUND OUT SHE WAS RIGHT. OF COURSE, BY THEN IT WAS TOO LATE.

ONE DAY, THE ALIENS LANDED ON THE RANCH.

WHICH DISTURBED THE CHICKENS.

The Unwelcome Guest

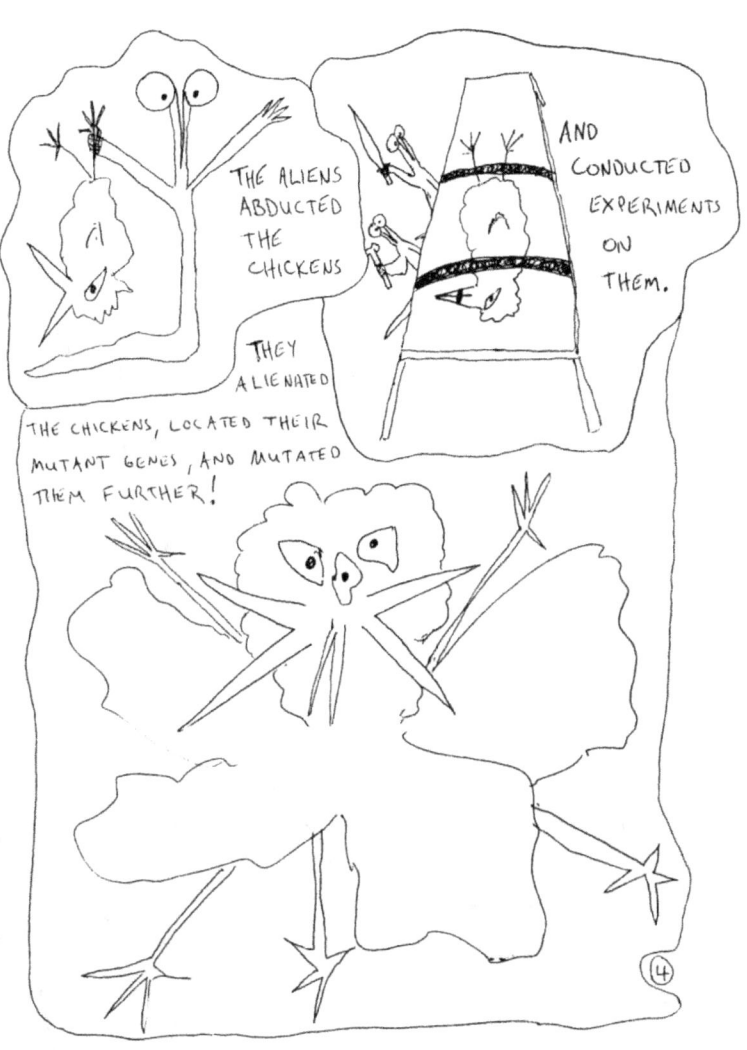

The Unwelcome Guest

FRED JAMESON WAS NOT AMUSED.

I FELT LIKE DRINKING HEAVILY

I FELT LIKE GOING FAR AWAY ACROSS THE SEA

I FELT SHEEPISH

MAYBE I COULD GET A JOB AS A SHEEP SHEARER

OR GO ON THE LAM

⑥

I WAS CANNED BECAUSE HE DIDN'T BELIEVE MY STORY. HE ALSO WOULDN'T LISTEN TO THE LADY FROM THE MIRROR STORE.

AND THEN DISTURBING REPORTS STARTED COMING IN FROM AROUND THE COUNTY, THEN FROM AROUND THE STATE, THEN FROM AROUND THE ENTIRE MIDWEST:

ALL MUTANT CHICKENS WERE DISAPPEARING

MUTANT CHICKEN ABDUCTION (M.C.A.) BECAME A CAUSE CELEBRÉ. ⑦

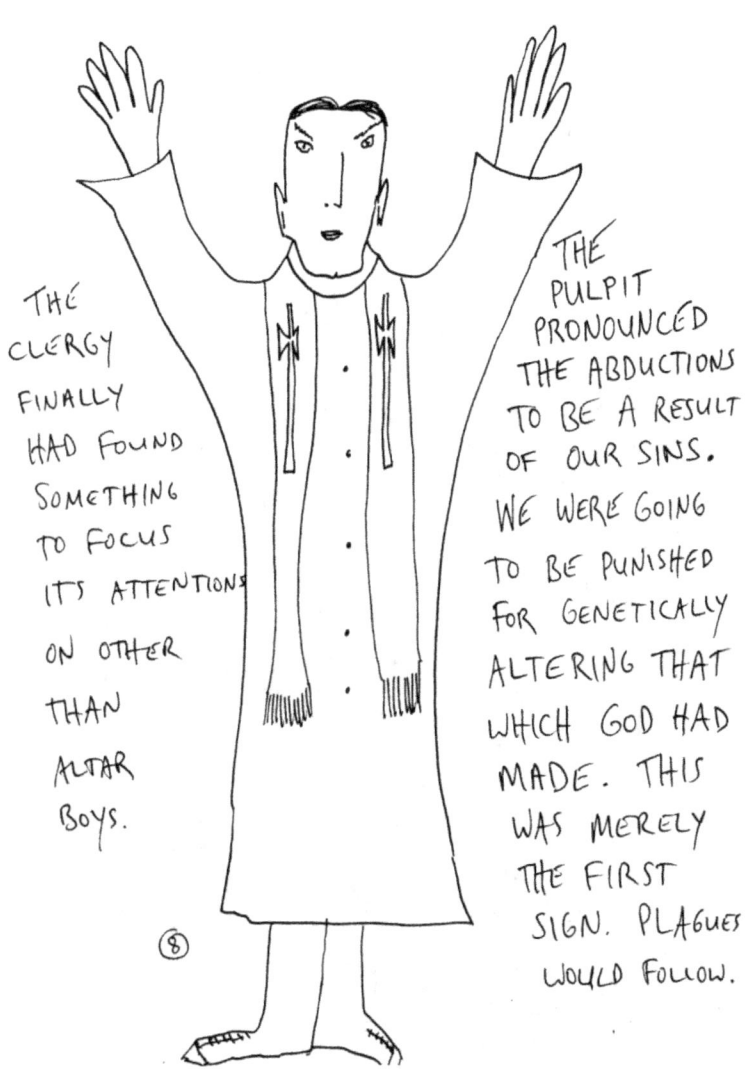

THE CLERGY FINALLY HAD FOUND SOMETHING TO FOCUS ITS ATTENTIONS ON OTHER THAN ALTAR BOYS.

THE PULPIT PRONOUNCED THE ABDUCTIONS TO BE A RESULT OF OUR SINS. WE WERE GOING TO BE PUNISHED FOR GENETICALLY ALTERING THAT WHICH GOD HAD MADE. THIS WAS MERELY THE FIRST SIGN. PLAGUES WOULD FOLLOW.

BUT THE GOVERNMENT'S RESPONSE
WAS PREDICTABLE:

I'm tired of bringing English to the nonbelievers. I am working out here on the backwoods mission, Green Acres Community College, and am forced into reading yet another batch of freshman composition essays. We English teachers must, on a very deep level, be coprophiliacs. Why else would we subject ourselves to such misery?

They stare at me with stupid bovine faces and tell me that they just *hate* English.

I tell them to learn another damn language, then. French is easier—only a tenth of the vocabulary. Spanish is pretty easy, I've heard. If they don't want to learn their mother tongue, they have plenty of other languages to choose from.

But instead of giving up, like a carpenter who only knows how to use a hammer, they give me their "in today's society" and their "needless to say" and their lame "in conclusion" and stupefy me—they bash in my brains with their misplaced modifiers, random punctuation, and ignorant disagreements.

I've been dreaming about another school—a huge urban research university, with buildings the size of cathedrals and castles. I am called to the central cathedral for faculty orientation. The cathedral has dozens of entrances and exits that lead to stairwells and passageways that criss cross like in some MC Escher drawing. People are filing in from all of them. We assemble haphazardly, still milling and babbling, and are told where our classes are and when. My first class is to meet in a half hour. I have never heard of the building I am to teach in. I head towards a stairwell and walk down it to an exit, open the large exterior door, only to discover a narrow field that stretches off to the left. People are filing that way, but a few hundred yards down, marauders appear out of the woods and begin slaughtering everyone. I escape back into the building and try to find another exit. Instead, I am back in the cathedral. I see a colleague I recognize from last year, which had been my first. He begins heading down another stairwell. I ask him if that's the way out. He says that he's convinced that each leads down into some sub-level of one's own consciousness. He's gone. I return to the cathedral to get my bearings, but then decide to follow him. When I retrace my steps, I find that the one stairwell is now four. I descend one, but end up at a train station. I get on the train, thinking that at least once I get down-town, I'll be able to get my bearings. The train descends, and its tracks lead us over and along a slime-green river. We descend into the river, and I realize I am not on a train anymore. I hear a voice saying that that had been a diffi-cult shot to get—that he'd had to suspend the camera from a helicopter by wires and then lower it into the river as it was moving. The view comes up out of the river, and I am deposited in the shopping district. Here I find the underground mall, which leads me to an exit near the school. I need to climb up terraced slumyards unnoticed to approach one of the school's peripheral buildings, which happens to be the faculty dorm to which I've been as-signed. My colleagues are inside smoking and eating silver hot dogs. One, an older man, is surprised to see me. "Aren't you supposed to be teaching tonight?" he asks.

I am decommissioned now.

Worms of Wisdom

Edwin Lubjec Thoth reported my existence as a government operative to the school newspaper, a psilocybin-run experiment called *My Colle' Tree*. Being whacked-out kids, they bought the conspiracy theory wholesale. I quickly fabricated a family emergency and resigned.

The G-men said, "Move away from there." They said, "California is the place you ought to be, so load up your truck and move to Menifee." They figured Thoth's arms didn't reach this far west. Just to be safe, though, they kept me far away from L.A. and San Diego. I was moved into a new subdivision in what once had been wine country. Of course, with me there, it was still wine country, but that's irrelevant.

I was given a Stewart tartan tie, but I wasn't sure if I should tie it in a Windsor knot or not, and the only knot I know is the double Windsor, so I was dubiously dumbfounded.

Thoth, I was told, tied his in a Gordian knot, which was a clue that would allow me to see through his Protean projections.

The question was raised by some asking whether or not Thoth was *the* Projectionist. No, the reply came—he was merely *a* projectionist. However, from what I was told, I surmised that tangelo was one of his preferred colors for his ties. I knew what to look for, but I wasn't sure whom to trust. I wasn't sure how Lubjec had escaped the police shooting that had allegedly killed him. Perhaps he'd gone on some Möbius trip and survived his sundering by becoming twice as large. Of course, if he'd become stronger in some ways, he must have correspondingly become weaker in others. I had to find those weaknesses.

Thoth had a habit of showing up where I'd least suspect him, so I decided to "cut him off at the pass," as they say in Westerns. I decided to first look where I'd least suspect. Remembering Poe's "Purloined Letter," I decided I should first look in my home.

I found crumbs on my kitchen counter. The shoes in my closet were mismatched. One of my t-shirts was hung up inside out. I couldn't find my paperback atlas of the world. And a match was missing from the matchbook in my bathroom cabinet drawer. I became suspicious that Thoth was somehow coming into my home when I was asleep or gone, so I changed my locks.

I had heard from an investigator once that he'd remembered that Thoth was in Mansfield Penitentiary. "You can get ahead at the Mansfield Pen," he said. "A decapitated head."

I wondered if that was how Thoth had escaped. Like the obscure version of Captain Marvel, he'd just say, "Split!" and his body would separate into five parts: limbs, head and torso. Each could find its own way out of the pen. Like Cistern Tawdry. Like a rolling stone. Like effluvium. Like a siamang. Like bebeeru. Daffy Dean. Matt Helm. And Bozo. Dig it. No weed like you do with angels coming. Your finer self is full of crap, and Mothra comes to exterminate you, grubs spraying, worms of wisdom—shut up, you! Shut up, you! Shut up, you! Shut up, you! Shut up, you! Grubs spraying, worms of wisdom. Shut up, you!

They were just crumbs in my kitchen, crumbs in my kitchen. Open my vein! I'll bet you'll think I'm betting against you. Won't you? Won't you? Mothra went up to the Mansfield Pen to see the total éclair of the shunned. I had whipped cream for their coffee, but they were just crumbs in my kitchen, crumbs in my kitchen.

"All right! Out, you crumbs! You heard the lady! And Mothra, don't forget this grub of yours. Where's the other one? Hey, anyone? Has anyone seen Mothra's other grub? Ah—there it is, snackin' off the kitchen floor. No surprise there—there's a week's worth of food spilled all over the floor. It cost over a thousand bucks. Why should mere mortals consume it? Oh, no—let's give the good stuff to the grubs!"

Like the leeches in the hospital whom we feed precious human blood all in the name of the reduction of swelling, we don't care about the reduction of swelling. We just want to feed the leeches. I found that out as a young orderly. I had no where to go—I was homeless, but the hospital staff did not know that, so I would find odd rooms to hide in and sleep or shower in when I was off duty. I was able to find a forgotten engineering room behind a false wall. I brought a perfectly okay TV up from the repair shop and was able to stay there undetected for a long time. During that time, on a nocturnal scouting mission, I found the leeches. They looked like they'd been placed in tanks with amputated limbs and freshly removed internal organs. I would have done more to investigate, but that night a medical delivery came to the hospital—an enormous truckload of drugs and supplies. An intern went from department to department, cleaned out all the tills, and paid the trucker for the delivery. Cash. Almost a quarter of a million dollars. Can you believe that? So the clamps came down. Security swarmed the building and found my nook but never connected me to it. But I could no longer sleep there, so I also lost interest in working there. I just stopped showing up. I knew of easier places to live.

The library, for example. Except my son could be a problem. One time I was in a hurry to get to the main floor and leave, so I took escalator after escalator from the living quarters on the top floors past the restaurants and stores on the middle floors to the second floor exit in the library, which one would walk through to get to the final escalator down to the street. My son, by going slow, got lost behind me twice. The second time, I went back to look for him, without success. He could have been outside alone for an hour and I wouldn't have noticed. I'm not always observant when I'm in a hurry. He finally came back, but I was scared. So scared that I had to find a secluded spot in the upper floors of the library to have a beer to calm myself. No sooner had I found that spot, in a corner of never-read antiquarian phonetic texts, then someone remarked, "Look! They're fighting!" and pushed past me to look out the window in that corner. On the adjacent rooftop, a couple of stories below, five or six women were arguing. One, with enormous sores on her face, yelled at another about "stealing" her "man." The yelled-at one was the flabbiest of the women and reached over one of her two defenders, who were also yelling, and landed a fist in the face of the one with sores, who dropped to the roof tar like a bundle of shingles. A crowd had gathered by the window. I wouldn't be able to drink my beer there. Damn! Come on, I said to my son, and we went to the literary criticism collections to see if I could drink my beer unnoticed there.

Then I wondered if Thoth might not be that shared man the women were arguing over. I smiled. That'd mean that he was diseased and dying already. That he had a penchant for gummatous women was interesting. A weakness I could maybe exploit sometime.

Driving down the street, I saw his name on a marquee: "Lubjec Live!" He was singing pop songs and playing guitar in a seedy redneck bar in Macon, Georgia. He covered his balding head with an oil-stained seed company baseball cap, wore rubber flipflops, and stomped his flipflops as he sang lovely country and pop standards like "Either a Redneck or a Deadneck," "I'll Push you Down into Low Places," "Oh Why Oh Why Ohio?" and the sure-to-get-'em hootin' crowdpleaser "My Baby's Been Knocked Up, So I'm Gonna Steal Me 800 Bucks."

The whole fucking bar starting singing the song, and then, on cue, they all turned to me like zombies and when they sang "800 Bucks," they held their hands out and started walking towards me.

"I'll be your friend," said one. "Give me 800 bucks."

"I'll be your friend," said another. "Give me 800 bucks."

I didn't know these people at all, but I had once loaned Lubjec 800 dollars for a demo he was going to cut with a band. Ironically, he used it, instead, to cut his unborn son out of his girlfriend's womb. Just like the song. And then the band broke up, and he never repaid me. He wouldn't even return my calls. Nor did he continue to pursue my friendship.

When he saw me walking in, he must have told these zombies I was an easy mark. If you're ever in Macon, be careful. The zombies live in the sewers, and Lubjec's people are the gatekeepers. Don't plumb to *their* depths.

Now that I think about it, I wish I had given them all 800 bucks so that they could have eliminated an entire generation of themselves. Someone needs to break the chain of two-faced back-stabbing thieving conniving sneaky manipulating weasels most of them are, spewing, "Oh, ain't you just *so* nice" in your face while they hold their pointed tails and pitchforks behind their backs where you can't see. Lubjec's their new hope, or was at least. They killed off Otis Redding and Duane Allman and Berry Oakley. They ran Little Richard out on a rail. They threw James Brown in jail. And then, all of a sudden, booming international music metropolis Macon, who'd hosted Cher and Iron Butterfly and Martin Mull and dozens of other internationally known artists, given them homes and re-cording contracts and made them stars, was suddenly empty. Real estate tycoons brought in cherry trees and paid for huge birthday parties for themselves in the city streets, but ruses and rubes couldn't replace what had been lost. Macon lost rock and roll and became a city of beasts that fuck themselves. And they have barbed pricks like raccoons, so you can hear them scream. And the screaming sounds like 5000 Chuckie dolls all singing in unison, "Whatcha gonna be, either a redneck or a deadneck?

Yew got no other option round here. You gonna be a red-neck or a flyspeck? If yer the ladder, stay out of my beer."

Twang twang twang twang. Scream!

You'd think they'd go through a ton of Excedrin in Ma-con—I did—but apparently they have no actual use for it there.

Amid the exhaustingly sweet-glazed billboards be-tween there and here are interjected proclamations of transcendence: Biblical warnings, certainly, but others much subtler: "The last umbrella you'll ever own," for ex-ample.

Why? Will the rain cease to fall? Will I drop dead when I open it? Unwilling to broadcast my ignorance. I try to avoid what I can. I imagine these transcendent proclama-tions a type of alien creature sent to disrupt our freeways. The proclamations begin to address this concern: Remove the feathers from your eyes! Use these coins instead. They grow into enormous unstable currencies. Don't end it with humor, no matter how the highway howls. The rain falls only on the highway. Climb the hills. Look out on the land. When it looks back, you've reached your destination. Don't be late for the time-share presentation! Employ-ment is shifting away from the highway and heading for the caves. Blast 'em open! Why not? Your head is your leader. The leader wants more coins!

Chevy Chase picked up the beers and Dan Aykroyd Tim Robbins brought the weed. We drove to the lake, got drunk and stoned, sat in the trees, threw rocks into the water, and did nothing. They, of course, knew each other better than they knew me, though I'd become a good friend recently.

Chevy'd pick me up and always had beers for the drive and then we'd get Dan Tim. Dan Tim would roll a bomber one-handed and we'd smoke it in the car on the way to the lake. We found a service shack and stored more beer in there.

They'd jab at each other a little. Chevy would make fun of the time Dan Tim was married to Farrah Fawcett. Or maybe it was Dan Tim making fun of Chevy. It didn't matter. It wasn't serious. No coins were blasted here.

During the cocaine era, Edwin used to call himself "L.T." for "Lubjec Thoth" but also in homage to his favorite cocaine-snorting linebacker. Briefly L.T. was big in celebrity circles and was even Bill Murray's ex-roommate. L.T. and I were living and working in an enormous space inside a mall. The space was filled with what we thought was a bookstore, though in truth the store was as tiny as a 31-Flavors shop, and our selection was only slightly more extensive. Mostly we sold bestsellers on discount.

We needed the rest of the space for our elaborate living quarters, with its wine cellar and separate suites. We had a large communal living room across a small false hall from the store's false back door. Here we'd relax and entertain while one of us minded the shop.

L.T. was a tall, balding classical guitarist with great talent but an insufficient sense of vocation to go anywhere with his music. His gawky awkwardness gave him a fragility on stage that would have translated into great success had he used it. Women saw this in him and surrounded him eagerly, hoping to be the ones to loose his potential. None of them did, and he never to my knowledge took unfair advantage of their enamorations.

The store was ostensibly owned by St. Izzy's High School, but was ignored by it for the most part, except when semesters were beginning. A trade bookstore in a mall receives substantially higher discounts on books than a text bookstore does, so the school was able to profit sufficiently from the discount difference.

That all these women would come in to see L.T. and he wouldn't do anything about it would bother me. The prettiest of them, Angie, was always hanging around. I liked Angie, but her sister was more interesting. Whereas Angie was perfect in every regard except she was somewhat shortchanged in the thinking department, Amelia was funny-looking, with a big nose, goofy hair, and Mick Jagger lips, but she was smart. She read William Gass and could hold conversations about real writers.

Unfortunately, Amelia was dating a low-life named Vlad, whose greatest ambition was to take apart a carburetor and reassemble it, and who treated Amelia terribly. But he took her attentions, and I was left pretty much unnoticed. Which meant I stayed at the register more than L.T.

Well, one day, while L.T. was in back with Angie, probably just talking, the fool, Duggan came in the store, right when it was really busy and I had a long line. Duggan was a bad boy legend from St. Izzy's. As a senior he had set off a pipe bomb in a bathroom and had blown off half of the face of some freshman. But Duggan's dad was a congressman, so nothing ever happened to Duggan.

It'd always been my instinct to hate him. This time, he picked up seven or so books, piled them on the counter and said to me he had a faculty discount. I almost choked. I knew there was no way in Christendom that the school had hired him as a teacher. I couldn't imagine Duggan ever even finishing high school.

"No," I said to him, staring him in the eye. "You're not on faculty."

He was about to argue, but the line of customers was so long I took the next one over him and rang her up. Duggan picked up his books and backed away to make room for her.

Two customers later, I realized Duggan and the books were both gone. I told my customer and the line to excuse me, and I went back to get L.T. to cover for me so I could comb the mall for Duggan.

L.T. went out front, sniffing about it, but, just as I was about to leave, Amelia came into the back area. I thought she wanted to see Angie, but Amelia pushed me right back into my suite. She started telling me about how she knew I'd always liked her, and she took my head in her hands and tried to kiss me. I had no idea what had come over her, but the idea of Duggan's getting away crowded her out. "I have to go," I told her. "I've got to catch a shoplifter. Wait here." I headed out toward the exit, hoping to find him, and there was Duggan, detained in conversation. Just then, I saw another St. Izzy's alumnus coming into the mall, none other than L.T.'s old roommate and Duggan's old classmate, movie star Bill Murray. "Bill!" I yelled. "Get Duggan! He hasn't paid!"

Murray looked around and saw Duggan. Duggan was trying to weasel his way out of there, but Murray and I were upon him in an instant. "Duggan," I said, "you have two choices. You pay for these books or you can go to jail right now."

Duggan paid and was on his way. Murray and I went out of the mall and sat on the lawn for a while and decompressed.

I asked him about his years at St. Izzy's and told him about mine, about how I got a job on the radio station so I could get out of Latin and how I'd go up on the roof and smoke pot and listen to old Genesis and Martin Mull and Allman Brothers records. I told him about my novels, and he asked me which my worst was.

I told him about *A Million-Year Centipede*, my first, which was about my visit to the Morrison Hotel in L.A. on the seventh anniversary of Jim Morrison's "death." I figured Morrison had thought of L.A. as "the land of the fair and the strong and the wise."

Just then, we heard a helicopter overhead. Murray's mom, a helicopter pilot, was hovering over us. She lowered a rope ladder to us, and we climbed it up to the helicopter. This helicopter had a truck bed and auxiliary wings for emergency gliding, and it was to these auxiliary wings that we strapped ourselves.

She took off and spun the chopper. I was amused for a while, but then I noticed my straps were loose. I climbed out of my straps and up into the truck bed.

The Unwelcome Guest

Murray's mom stopped spinning and took us back to the house/store/mall.

Some time passed, and I was in the living room with Amelia, holding her on the couch while we watched a movie on TV. L.T. and Angie were there, too. The store had closed for the night.

Murray was in the hallway, and we could see him. He showed us a blue steel plate picture he had of a dancing girl in a grass skirt. He began nailing the plate to the store's false front. As we was hanging it, he began singing, "Oh, she's come home, for she's an evil sculpture! Ah, hah! Oh, she's come home..."

Credits roll. The end.

Thoth is a bare-assed baboon whose name, ironically, means "the learned one." He's learned how to show off his red ass, that's all.

He was playing on our church-league soccer team once when he drew two yellow cards, both for smarting off at the referee. Of course, with the second card he earned a red card as well and was ejected. He pulled down his shorts and gave the ref his own red calling card. He was suspended for the season for that.

I wondered how he got it so red. Did he use sandpaper to wipe with? Was he still being spanked? He deserved a nail-studded two-by-four across the head, not a little paddling of the bum.

That little pudding of a brain that stirs around in Lubjec congeals itself around the topic of betrayal of a friend. Betrayal is his raison d'être. His sins are not important. They are ubiquitous. Whatever he said was too good for us. He tried so very hard to get us to see the truth. He endured us, we whose writing is merely means to an end.

Yes! *His* end! If you see this base turd on the road, squash him with your oxfords. How erudite he will seem then, Mr. I-Was-Too-Smart-to-Waste-My-Time-at-College-Because-I-Had-Already-Been-Offered-a-Six-Figure-Job-Holding-My-Thumb-Down-on-the-Boss's-Chair-so-He-Could-Sit-on-It-Whenever-He-Pleased, Mr. I-Love-Big-Business-Especially-the-Big-Oil-Companies-Because-I-Suck-Too, Mr. I-Spread-Mayonnaise-on-the-Chrome-of-My-Car's-Rear-Bumper.

His biography will be entitled *To Please the Boss*. You've heard of people who don't know up from down? I tell you Lubjec actually thought "the Netherlands" was a reference to Hell. As a Frisian, I have problem with that. And I presume his God is something like Ned Beatty in the movie *Network*. What seemed like impossibly strange prophecy then is our current commonplace reality now. The corporations control the nations, the media makes the news, and the corporations own all media. Everything is a commodity.

Lubjec worked as an advertising photographer for years. He created images on command, images designed to hoodwink the unalert. And who can remain alert for long in this world? Televisions, billboards, magazines, radios all thumping us, bashing our heads in until we submit, knocking us unconscious so we can be fed subliminally. And the controllers have us thanking them for having pounded us into oblivion: We foolishly believe the oblivion to be freedom, a release from their control, but even there they have lined the streets with their billboards. Dante is nothing more than a brand name now. Didn't Dante write all the Archies' songs? Ah, ha!

Maybe Lubjec is right. Perhaps there's no real joy in life. Life is nothing but people hurting each other until they die. The only truly free person is the person who is free of hope. We are misery. Only the insane and deluded could think otherwise.

Should I cast my lot with the insane and deluded? Should I hold onto the iron life-raft that is hope? Or should I wake up and realize that the abuse that is heaped on me is more than richly deserved? I deserve worse. I am the miserable cretin. Lubjec is merely a realist. I resent his honesty. It interferes with my fantasy of a life that is worth living. I'm a chump.

I am the em-bare-assed baboon. Do I now hold sufficient wisdom to survive this world? Or am I just another cracked vessel? A crack pot, as folks used to say before they meant different things by "crack" and "pot." Or did they? Thoth is truth. Thought is not. Blind obeisance and total resignation to the will of our corporate leaders is the only permissible response. Look around yourself— commodities are facing you right now! Rush out and buy whatever it is that's being advertised! Now!

Or: reject the unwelcome guest who comes to occupy your head.

Endgames

Edwin became a filmmaker for a year when he received an unexpected, jokingly-applied-for federal grant. In return, he was to produce three short propaganda films for the political party in power. The films were to depict attempted assassinations of the party leader. The propaganda was designed to depict resistance to despotism as traitorous. Each film depicted one of the three largest minority groups organizing in armed resistance. The minorities, one would assume, were building an unholy triumvirate and would carve up the body of the leader and feed him to their dogs.

These films would instill enough fear in the commoner that the commoner would embrace the leader again and despise instead the plotting minorities. The films were successful, and violence against these minorities doubled in the cities. The leader retained his hold on his office.

When Thoth is dead, we'll peel the film from his eyes. That way we can see what he saw. Various federal agents have been by, looking for Thoth. When the President himself came by, some stupid redneck song, "Drown in the Chattahoochee," came on the radio. I smiled at the coincidence.

I told them all, "I hope you get him."

The last two agents seemed particularly bright and good-natured. They returned later to tell me they'd gotten Thoth.

"Good," I said. "It was inevitable." I watched the three of them, Thoth in shackles, walk away through the tall grass, back up to the locked gate by the highway. Too bad they wouldn't be able to hold him, I thought. Drown him in my pond, Pause Lake. Hecho en USA. I'd have to sell the property of course, now that everyone knew where it was and connected it to good o' Chattahoochee Edwin. Oh, well.

I was free of him for a while immediately thereafter. I moved, got a job as a night watchman at a resort, and was left alone. I had a radio, books to read, and a putt-putt course. My first night, I remember, I scored a 58 for 18 holes. Take that, Edwin! His golf obsession was legendary. Here I was practicing my putting game every night and getting paid for it! That made me a professional, right? It was the perfect job for an insomniac isolationist like me. My gasping for air because of my sleep apnea would no longer disturb my wife's sleep. Nor would my snoring.

Dad wouldn't be grumpy in the morning when my kids woke up because by then I'd be home and have had a couple of beers already, and then I'd be asleep. I'd still have afternoon time and supper with my wife and kids. But what was attractive was I'd never have to deal with Lubjec, who was certainly diurnal.

I asked him if he'd golf with me once, years ago. He laughed and said, "You're just a beginner. Why would I waste my time golfing with a beginner? Take some classes or something and tell me when you break 80." I assume he meant for 18. What an ass. What a bare-assed baboon! I already had a 58! And a 62 later that night! That's 120 for 36 holes! In one night! I don't want to hear about breaking 80 ever again!

My second night at the resort I brought several crossword puzzles. I had completed the Sunday *Los Angeles Times* puzzle the night before, and I enjoyed it. The second night I tried the *New York Times* Sunday puzzle, but it was much more heavily drawn from pop culture than the L.A. one. The L.A. paper had more history and geography questions, which I'm better at. I don't know much about Broadway stars or TV divas. I shot a 57 at 1:30 in the morning. Those poor suckers who wake up at 5:30 only to shoot an 80—what slobs! What rank amateurs!

My second round that night I shot a 59, but I had a 25 on the front nine. Fifteen hung me up—I started getting back spasms and double-bogeyed the hold and then bogeyed sixteen. I had to forego the third round that I'd been planning on. Normally, 54 holes shouldn't be a problem.

Meanwhile, Lubjec had kept himself busy. I saw him on the news. Daniel Noriega was giving a press conference, and there, right behind Noriega's left shoulder, stood a bespectacled, bearded Lubjec. Whether he was working toward Noriega's overthrow or against, I have no idea. Lubjec may not even have known himself. When I was an industrial operative with Lubjec, that's the way it was— after a while we had no idea if we were working for or against our employer. I suppose you could say we did both. Lubjec, especially. He'd volunteer to birth a cow and then deliver a stillborn. He'd help roofers carry squares up a ladder, but then he'd kick the ladder away.

I figured it out when we played chess. He had no endgame. He would attack, and if black, he'd overtake. But he lacked a final plan. Frequently, even if he was ahead by a couple of good pieces, I could stalemate him by getting him on the run. His essential flaw was, perhaps, that he was purely reactive. One could bank on it.

My third night on the job I recorded a 66 and a 59. I had back spasms, though. I had a 24 on the front nine on my second round. The first round of 66 I put off to the incredible distractions. I was working on a Friday night, an entire YMCA fellowship was occupying one of the four camping areas, and people kept coming by the guard shack to get their assigned campsites. The nerve of some people! Couldn't they see I was golfing? I took some painkillers and decided to try a third time shortly before dawn. My third, round, though, also yielded a 59. I had a 52 going into 18, but my spasms were so bad that I got a 7 on that last hole. Perhaps my endgame's not so good as Beckett's either.

The fourth night the fifth hole led into a periscope of a decommissioned Russian submarine. A frightened old man was on the other side. His wild white sideburns quivered when I asked him about Lubjec. He placed an exploding scone on the sixth tee and blew himself up with his driver rather than answer my questions. Perhaps I was getting close to the truth. When the brine flooded the sub, I knew I was in a pickle. I figured this was a hell of a way to lose weight.

I made my way to the surface and began to notice my sentence structure. Fragments everywhere. Was it true that Lubjec existed only on paper?

Debriefed by the naval officers who picked me up, I felt naked. My pen was taken from me and broken.

I saw Ed...win.

I was sunk. I was bottled in, and I was in the drink.

I was the gin djinn, and only the reading of my tale would let me out. So, Lubjec, what will you do with me now?

Nin
&
Nan

Chapter One: The Sign

Nin and Nan sat at the top of the hill together and ob-
served the goings-on below. Nin's mind was sufficiently
empty. Nan's was insufficiently so. The future was never
not far enough away. Enough that neither of them would
never know.

Nin liked straw. Nan liked Styrofoam. The hill obviously
disliked the straw because the hill did all it could to free
itself of the itchy stuff: it begged the winds to come and
blow it away, it enraged the fireflies and it shook itself
fiercely. It didn't mind Styrofoam, which was just fluff, but
everyone else did, especially the bugs who came to rest on
the hill, and because the bugs were such terrible whiners,
the hill decided not to tolerate Styrofoam either.

Nin said to Nan that one fateful morning, "Look—

beans are encroaching upon our hill."

Nan looked around. True—the beanfields seemed much closer than they had just a few months earlier.

"No, not those beans," said Nin, pointing to the beanfields. "*Those* beans." Nin pointed at a newly constructed billboard alongside the not-too-distant highway.

Nan at first did not see it and imagined a different billboard: "Coca Beans—put some toot in your toot!" But Nan quickly dismissed the idea as too silly to even mention to Nin, and by then Nan saw the offending blot on the landscape, a billboard so enormous and gaudy that why Nan hadn't previously noticed it was worthy of some psychological investigation perhaps. But that would have to wait for another time, for at the time the only item being investigated was the billboard: a fifty-foot wide by twenty-foot tall luminescent green-and-pink lettered atrocity featuring a photo of a smiling, dancing string bean in top hat, tails, cane, can and spats. The bean was ascending a spiral staircase. The advertisement text read, "Dance up a stair to good health with Rogers' brand beans."

"Oh, that has to come down, Nin," said Nan.

"Exactly, Nan," replied Nin.

Nan rolled down the hill, across the highway and along the shoulder up to the billboard. Fortunately, it was cheaply constructed of soft pine. That gave Nan an idea for the moral justification for the destruction of the sign.

Back up the hill, Nan said, "Nin, they've killed the trees that went into the manufacture of that sign."

"True, Nan."

"And they've drained the trees of their life energy."

"True again, Nan."

"Would it be wrong... wouldn't it indeed be a holy thing for us to restore to the trees their energy?"

"Yes, indeed."

"And what are the spirits of pine called?"

"Why, turpentine, Nan. We have some at home."

"Yes, we should get it."

"Yes, and then we'll soak the sign in the spirits of pine and restore the life energy."

"Yes."

"But Nan?"

"Yes, Nin?"

"That may not be enough. For this to be a *holy* transformation, we need more. Do you remember the holy transformation of Christ's disciples?"

"Of course, Nin. The Pentecost."

"Wasn't the spiritual transformation described as taking place in tongues of fire? Hasn't it been depicted so by artists for centuries?"

"Ah, yes! So after we douse the sign, we must ignite it with the spirit of the Lord."

"Yes, Nan. You get the turpentine. I'll get the matches."

When Nin lit the fire, Nan was reminded of Abednego's surviving the flames of Nebuchadnezzar's furnace in Babylon. From the German *abend*, or "evening"; the English "a-bed," meaning "to take oneself to bed"; the Hebrew *neg*—, meaning "south" [to the Hebrews, of course, the black races lived south]; and the Latin *nec*, meaning "not," a statement of contrast. Abednego's surviving the flames contrasted the darkness of night yet also upheld it. That it was both things contradictory simultaneously was inherent. All things confirm their opposites. The atheist is as dependent upon the concept of God for hir (i.e. "his or her") self-definition as the theist is. By standing In opposition to theism, the atheist acknowledges the existence of theism. Indeed, the atheist *needs* the existence of theism in order to exist hirself.

Of course, unlike Abednego, the billboard did not emerge from the fire unscathed. Coca the dancing string bean shriveled and writhed as the bill separated from the board. The wood was freed to dance according to its grain, and as Nin and Nan watched, it danced itself away completely. The billboard turned dark as it was consumed by fire, and then, in turn, fire gave way to the darkness of night. The spiritual transformation of the wood was complete. Nin and Nan watched the last embers give way before returning to the home inside the hill.

Chapter Two: The Road

Days passed, and Nin and Nan enjoyed the return of the landscape to the state it had been in before it had the sign: the purples, yellows, reds and blues of the wildflowers on the heath, punctuated by thickets of gnarled black oaks, weeping willows, scarlet buckeyes, and Eastern cottonwoods, and connected by a two-lane road that reticulated through the countryside like an unwelcome python. The hiss and smoke from the occasional automotive parasites crawling along its skin was repulsive. Both host and parasites had to go.

"We should do something about those pesky cars," said Nin, pointing again.

Nan expected to see a billboard advertising automobiles. A celebrity, perhaps, someone like Imogene Cocabean, holding open the driver's side door to the newest Studebaker, the Studebaker Hawk, and welcoming the viewer into the seat. And something lewd to connect image and purpose—a double entendre: "Come inside," perhaps.

"Where?" Nan asked Nin. No new signage had been put up to replace the obliterated one. The liberated one, that is.

In the distance, a dark Lincoln Continental was approaching. Even at a distance, it seemed to be moving quickly.

"I don't think we'll be able to catch it, Nin. It's moving too fast."

"True, Nan. And to be fair, they wouldn't even be

coming along here if there were no road for them to travel on."

"I agree. But we can't get rid of the entire road, can we? It's not as easy as a billboard."

"You are correct that it won't be easy, but I know we have to do it."

They sat quietly, gathering their thoughts.

"Nin?"

"What, Nan?"

"I know why we have to do this."

"Why, Nan?"

"Because the road is a false god, and we must tear down all false idols."

"Exactly!"

"Jesus said, 'I am the way,' but the road pretends *it* is the way."

"*Via* in Latin can mean 'road' or 'path' or 'way,' so you are correct, Nan."

"But how can we remove a road without being noticed?"

"Like Hadrian said: 'One brick at a time,' Nan. We must determine the vanishing points on either horizon and begin there, gradually removing a narrow strip of pavement from alongside the shoulder and then, eventually, from the road. This way, gradually, the road will become narrower and narrower until it just ceases to exist."

"But, Nin, do we have a maul?"

"Yes, we do."

"Do we have a spade?"

"Yes."

"Do we have a wheelbarrow?"

"Yes."

"Okay, so let's go find the road's horizons."

On one end, the road came over a hill and was lined by huge willows on both sides. At the other, the road vanished into a valley between two hills dotted with enormous granite boulders. The road's sacrilegious alpha and omega had been easier to define than Nin had anticipated. Very good, thought Nin.

They began mauling and shoveling the road into the wheelbarrow. Load after load they carted off over the horizon and buried in a field. Many days, weeks and months were spent by Nin and Nan in this pursuit. They were vigilant and successfully avoided detection by all occasionally passing cars.

Nan figured they had moved enough wheelbarrow loads and carried them far enough that, if the moved material were laid lengthwise in a one-inch wide strip, it could from where they were reach Point Barrow, Alaska.

Nin said, one day, "Every time we finish a strip, the road seems just as wide as before."

Nan replied, "Remember St. Cyril of Jerusalem's famous Parable of the Holy Trinity."

Nin asked, "No—what was that?"

Nan said, "In the 4th century, St. Cyril wrote that St. Augustine was walking along the beach one day and met a child who had dug a hole in the sand and who kept carrying water from the ocean to the hole, only to see the water disappear. When Augustine asked the child what he was doing, the child said he was trying to put the entire ocean into the little hole. Augustine said to the child that it was impossible to fit the ocean into that little hole. The child replied that he'd be able to fit the ocean into the hole before St. Augustine would be able to explain the mystery of the Holy Trinity."

Other days saw Nin encouraging Nan not to despair. By bucking each other up, they finally saw the day come when they could see their progress. It was a day of joy, and that night they celebrated. They feasted and drank wine. The road was certainly more narrow than it had been!

They ordered a couple of "Road Narrows" signs for the horizons and placed them just beyond where they could see. This would avert the passing drivers' suspicions. Even the occasional trooper would suspect little more than an incompetent DMV. These signs would suffice until the road became too narrow for two-lane traffic. At that point, the "Road Narrows" signs were replaced with "One Lane Road Ahead" signs. When the road had narrowed to within that proportion, the signs were replaced with signs stating, "Road Closed for Repair," and a week later, with railings and "Road Ends" signs. Exhausted but satisfied, Nin and Nan collapsed into their hill and slept for the better part of a week.

Chapter Three: A Visitor

Nin's and Nan's surprise was not altogether unsuspected when one day they saw a Range Rover churning up dust along the former road.

"What do you think he's up to, Nan?"

"I don't know, but we just finished seeding the ground. That meanie is undoing our work."

"Do you think it might be a revenuer?"

"Oh. You mean like Daddy used to shoot?"

"Yes."

"What do you think he wants?"

"Only two things the government ever wants, Nan: money or land."

"Heck, we don't have any money, Nin."

"Then I guess he's coming for our land."

"But this isn't even our land. It's God's land."

"I think he'd say that the domain is *eminent*."

"What's that mean?"

"That means no one's allowed to own any land except the government."

"Even God?"

"Especially God."

"But God made all this."

"Sure, but the government wants what's God's."

"Aren't we supposed to render unto Caesar what is Caesar's and unto God what is God's?"

"Yes."

"So we've got to stop this revenuer, Nin."

"Yes, we do. Let's go out and meet him by the road."

"The garden, you mean."

"Of course. Sorry. The garden."

"Okay, Nin."

Nan felt angry that this revenuer was destroying the newly planted beds of melon, squash carrots, cabbage, lettuce, and radishes. Nin and Nan had worked hard on these after recovering from removing the road.

Nan jumped out in front the Range Rover, which turned sharply to avoid Nan and rolled onto its side. A furious bear of a man with a cut on his nose that was bleeding a river clambered out. He was wearing a ranger uniform.

Nan yelled at him, "You idiot! You're going through my vegetable garden! What are you doing?"

The ranger didn't seem to understand. He held up a finger as if to make a point and fell over dead. His brain had hemorrhaged.

Nin and Nan righted the Range Rover, pulled the ranger in, and then drove over the horizon. They jumped out just as the Range Rover and its occupant drove off a promontory point into the lake below.

They hurried back and wiped away the Range Rover's tracks. Nan spent the next two days re-seeding the dirt and swearing. Nin left Nan alone when Nan was like that. Nothing could have consoled Nan just then. The working of the dirt with fingers and replanting of seeds was therapy enough. And, for good measure, Nan also planted mustard seeds.

What worried Nin was that when one lone-wolf revenuer appeared, others were sure to follow close behind.

Nin & Nan

They always worked in packs. The lone wolf was sent like the right eye, and having offended, it was plucked out. But now the rest of the *corpus lupi* had to be dealt with.

Nin and Nan dug pits in which they stood up logs with sharpened ends. They covered these pits with sod. The next Range Rovers would be skewered before they knew what had hit them. The fact that the dirt had turned to sod and that enormous piles of dirt stood alongside the road and wouldn't even be noticed by the revenuers, who were notoriously stupid, was fascinating.

Actually, seventeen revenuers came by to inquire, but all met mysterious disappearances, all obviously incapable of learning from the vanishings of their predecessors.

Eventually the revenuers stopped coming. Nin and Nan relaxed, confident, celebrated.

Chapter Four: A Pied Piper Arrives

Uncle Sam pulls them along in a sling towed by giant razor-toothed clams. Or so went the song.

Nin and Nan listened to American music. They liked America. They just couldn't suffer her misrepresentatives' intrusions.

Musicians showed them a way to hear music as tastefully touching as they had sniffed it out to be.

Fanfare could have announced the approach of music but did not. Its arrival was sudden and surprising.

"Hullooo?" boomed a musical voice from outside of the hill one morning.

Waking up, Nin looked at Nan, and Nan looked at Nin.

"What in the realm of rowdy ratchets was *that*?" asked Nan.

"A visitor?"

"Not another revenuer, I hope."

"I don't think so. We haven't seen a revenuer in nearly a year. This must be something else."

"Like a gypsy?"

"Or a salesman. Or an evangelist for a mistaken cult."

"Why mistaken?"

"No true believer would ever be so hostile as to use direct confrontation at someone's home as an evangelistic tool. True evangelism cannot occur in a hostile climate. That's the whole principle behind the Rogerian Strategy."

"The what?"

"Carl Rogers's conflict resolution model for argument and persuasion. Rogers said that to reduce the sense of threat that prohibits people from considering your ideology, you must demonstrate that you have carefully considered and respect theirs. Only then might you get someone to agree to reciprocate by listening to you. That's why confrontational proselytizing always fails. Forced conversions are false con-versions."

"Hmm..."

"I remember going to the grocery store once. I was standing in the cereal aisle, trying to find a breakfast cereal without BHA or BHT, which are carcinogens, when I felt holes being bored into the side of my face by some stranger's stare from down the aisle. I turned and looked to see a bug-eyed fellow coming toward me. I knew he was either a religious zealot or a drug addict. In either case, I did not want to talk to him. But then, sure enough, he confronted me. Without so much as a 'by your leave,' he asked me if I'd accepted the Lord Jesus Christ as my personal savior."

"Did you tell him about your beliefs?"

"No! He wasn't interested in *my* beliefs! All he wanted was to force his own XYZ Brand of Christianity on me. You know what I said?"

"No."

"I said, 'Excuse me. Would you accompany me to the customer service desk so that I can have you thrown out of the store for harassing a customer?' Then he said, 'I'm not harassing you,' so I replied, 'Then shut up!' He had no chance in hell of converting me to XYZ Brand that way. If he'd been smart, he'd have asked me about the cereal boxes. He'd have talked to me for five hours about cereal boxes if I wanted before ever saying *anything* about XYZ

Brand."

"That's like what I read about W. Clement Stone, who wrote that *Success through a Positive Mental Attitude* book. He was an insurance salesman, and when he went on his rounds, he'd stop in at folks' houses and just talk to them about their families and such. You know—you have kids? You ever envision them going to college? Oh, really? Where? Mind if I ask you what you do for a living? And so on, never revealing once anything about himself. When his supervisors made follow-up phone calls to those folks later, you know—our man Stone was out there last week and we were wondering what your impression of him was—to a person these folks all said, 'Oh, Mr. *Stone*? He was delightful! What an interesting person!' But as I said, he never said anything about himself. What these folks found interesting, apparently, was themselves! They loved talking about themselves. Stone knew this and used this to entice them into wanting to reciprocate, which they could, of course, by buying a little piece of mind from him."

"Hullooo?" came the voice again.

"Should we let him in?" asked Nan.

"Yes, but be careful. Be on your toes. Don't tell him anything. He may work for the revenuers. They're everywhere, I tell you, and are just waiting for a chance to destroy us."

"Okay. We'll be very careful. No cult evangelist is going to fool us."

"Let him in, Nan."

"Certainly, Nin."

The man at the door was weird and had silver stars in

his long white beard. His shirt had white stars on a blue background, as did his duffel bag, and his loose pantaloons were pied red and white. His stovepipe hat swirled all four colors together. But he was barefoot.

Slung back over his shoulder was a folk guitar on a white silk strap. The strap had the initials "SRV" embroidered into it in silver thread.

"Couldn't stand the weather?" asked Nan, assuming the visitor to be a Stevie Ray Vaughn fan.

"Hulloo? Oh—the strap. My brother found it in an alley in Austin, Texas. It was a night when Jimmy Vaughn was playing with his brother's old band. Everyone said they could sense Stevie's presence that night, and then my brother, who tended bar there at Antone's, went outside for a smoke and spotted the strap. He brought it in and one of the guys in the band went pale and asked him where he'd gotten it. He said the alley. The band guy said that was spooky because it was Stevie's old strap."

Nan looked at Nin, "No Rogerian Strategy here, eh?"

Nin laughed. "Apparently not." He turned his attention to Uncle Sam. "What can we do for you?"

Nan's attention began to wander.

You know, at some point I stopped writing, and I started talking. Is this the epiphany I, as a Joycean, had set myself up for? Or am I delusional?

"..., so I'd be happy to play a song." Nan had missed the first half of the sentence, the cause in the causal connection. Without that, for all Nan knew, Nin and Nan could be facing a *post hoc ergo propter hoc* argument or a deceptive enthymeme or a nonsequitur. Unless the premise is true, the conclusion is invalid.

Nin was distracted by the strange look on Nan's face, and responded for them both: "Depends on the song."

Nin ushered Uncle Sam in, and Nan went to the fridge to get some Jesus' Own Brand cheap wine with a smiling half-crocked Jesus on the label, halo and all. In the famous TV commercial, Jesus would sing, "You gotta have J.O.B. if you wanna be with me."

"Halooo?" pointed out Uncle Sam, touching the label like God touching Adam's outstretched finger. To his credit, he shook his head and said, "No, don't drink."

Nan responded with, "Don't mind if I do," and poured two glasses. Nan handed one to Nin.

They clinked, and Nan said, "To the song! What song have you brought us, oh Elliptical One?"

"Elliptical One?"

"That's good, isn't it?"

"You just make that up?"

"Yep."

"Okay. Good. Keep going."

"Oh, Bringer of the Tune, we'd like to hear you soon."

Uncle Sam snapped to attention as if he'd forgotten he was part of the conversation and had been playing at being Strictly Silent Observer Man. I don't think he has a superhero complex.

"Okay," said Uncle Sam. "Here goes." He flipped his guitar around, pulled a pick out his pick pocket, and prestidigitated, but no sound came out for the longest time until a slight bell could be heard way far away, like a church in a blizzard, just barely audible. It began to shape

Nin & Nan

itself around a letter, a note...

Z. Buzz. By Uncle Sam

Z. Buzz. Z. Buzz. Z. Buzz.
Zeboombadoom!
Z. Buzz. Z. Buzz. Z. Buzz.
Zeboombadoom!

We send our bombs hailing down on you,
those of you in Sector Blue,
you who've been so gravel-blind (as to)
take Granny Smith for Gravenstein.

A. Smash! A. Smash! A. Smash!
Krackaragnarok!
A. Smash! A. Smash! A. Smash!
Krackaragnarok!

We saw the signs come down in flames
and the erasure of our agents' names.
We saw the road get taken down (by)
a modern James Gang, as they say in town.

Clickety snap! Clickety snap!
Cuff 'em! Read 'em their rights!
Then string 'em up from the highest tree!
We'll have peace in town tonight!

There'll be no deviation from our prescription.
The road will have to be rebuilt.

Kill the wrecking crew before they kill you.
Can't you see their guilt?

Snap swing swing swing! Snap swing!
Zeboombadoom!!
No one can stop us now
or tell us what to sing!

Death to our friends, our enemies!
Death to all we see!
Death to the infidel and to the god-fearing!
See them in that tree!

Z. Buzz. Z. Buzz. Z. Buzz.
Zeboombadoom!
Z. Buzz. Z. Buzz. Z. Buzz.
   Zeboombadoom

Uncle Sam had been singing since 11:55 a.m. By noon, nonconformists Nan and Nin knuckled under and announced that they could stand no more of his music.

"What kind of music was that?" asked Nin.

"I call it 'political satire,'" said Uncle Sam.

"No—it sounds more like propaganda," said Nan. "Redneck propaganda."

"Truly," said Nin, "you suck. Those were the lamest lyrics. What were all the goofy sounds? Did you want them to be onomatopoeia? Or is this a song for silly little children?"

"And the nitwits."

Uncle Sam looked offended. "Then which are you?

Children or nitwits?"

"Neither."

"Did you even *listen* to the lyrics? They're a warning."

"I heard enough to hear that they blow," said Nin.

"No no no—you need to *study* the lyrics!" replied Uncle Sam.

"No no *no*," said Nan, mockingly. "*You* need to go!"

"No, here. Here's a copy of my CD," and Uncle Sam opened his duffel bag. The odor of dirty laundry quickly filled the room. Nin saw dozens of CDs inside the bag besides the stinky clothing. Uncle Sam pulled out a peach-colored CD case with black lettering announcing its title: *CD for Nin and Nan*.

Nin realized that Uncle Sam's visit could not have been accidental.

"Why would we want your stinkin' CD?" asked Nan. Nin picked up the CD and showed the title to Nan.

"Hey, Brother Sam did this just for us."

"Oh, he just has a different cover for each copy he brings to each house."

"No," interjects Uncle Sam. "That's the actual title. I've sold dozens of them. Look," and he pulled dozen more of the same CD out of his bag.

"How much are you selling them for?"

"Only ten bucks."

"All right—give us one." Nin pulled a ten-spot out. "Here, Brother Sam. For your CD and your rap."

"Should I sign it?"

"Please. Sign it, but don't inscribe it," said Nin (whispering to Nan, "resale value!").

"A lyric sheet's inside," said Uncle Sam.

"Enough with the lyrics already," said Nan. "It's time to leave."

"Read the lyrics," Uncle Sam said, closing his duffel bag, flipping the guitar back over his shoulder and then picking up the duffel bag. "Thanks for the beer."

"You're welcome, Brother Sam," said Nin, guiding the "intruder" out the door.

"What an ass!" said Nan as soon as the door closed behind Uncle Sam. "Do you believe that song? Snickety-snack? Wasn't that a line from Lewis Carroll?"

"I think so. 'The Jabberwocky.'"

"And you! Why were you being so nice to him?"

"What do you mean, Nan?"

"Calling him 'Brother Sam'! My gosh!"

"Well, I figured if Uncle Sam is the U.S., then Brother Sam is the—"

"Oh, that *is* funny. But why did you buy the CD?"

"To get rid of him. Told you he'd be a salesman. That's all he wanted. So, ten bucks and now he's gone. That was simple, and relatively cheap. Imagine if he'd been a Bible Salesman ? We'd have spent ten times that."

"Yeah, because we like the Bible."

"Well, we'll give this a listen. Maybe it'll sound better all produced and slicked up."

"I hope so, because it reeked live."

"Okay, I'll put it on."

"Not *now*. We just survived it once. Let's regain our strength first," implored Nan.

"Oh, no. Then you'll never get around to it. I know you.

Now or never."

"Later. You can't catch me with a false dilemma."

"And you won't catch me with Big-Legged Emma."

"Zappa! That's right. Your Brother Sam doesn't seem to know Zappa."

"*My* brother? Fine. I don't care if we ever listen to the CD. Even if it *is* about *us*."

"Just *to* us, I think," said Nan.

"How do you know? What does 'skooby skippy' mean, or whatever he said? It could be an insult in his own personal secret language."

"Like *Magma*? What was their language? Kobaian?"

"I think so. That sounds right. But that's not what it was."

"You don't think so?"

"No—I'm pretty sure it was just scat."

"Scat? It *was* B.S.!"

"Ha! No," said Nin, laughing. "*Scat*! As in Scatman Crothers. Zippy de zow eye! He had a version of 'Be-Bop-A-Lula' that rocked! But he was big with scat singing!"

"Big scat? B.S."

"Oh, back to your Zappa with your potty humor, you!"

"Anyway, that crap of your Brother Sam's was no language. Heck, that fool didn't even speak his *own* language well," and then he added with a sarcastic snort, "Kobaian."

"Didn't Nirvana sing in Kobaian also?"

"No—that was Cobainian."

"Well, in both cases, the bands didn't care if anyone could understand the lyrics. So why do we have to?"

Chapter Five: The CD

Two weeks later, they still hadn't heard the CD. They were sitting around bored one afternoon when Nin asked, "What do you want to do?"

Nan absently replied, "Nothing particular. Anything you want is okay."

Nin leapt up and grabbed the CD case. "Ah, ha! In that case, we are *now* listening to this."

"No! I didn't mean I'd agree to *any*thing."

"Yes, that's precisely what you *did* say, and I'm holding you to it right now."

"Well, let's at least smoke some satistiva first."

"Okay. We can do that."

Nan rolled up a cigarette, and they shared it down to the end before Nin stood up and grabbed the CD case again. Nan was too stoned to object.

The CD player gave Nin a little trouble at first, but in a few seconds, the sound of a faint church bell tolling could be heard. Nin sat next to Nan on the couch and folded the lyric sheet open for them to read.

That's rather cliché, thought Nan. *He stole that from AC/DC.* And then the buzzsaw lyrics began. Bombs dropping. Okay. Got that. Sector Blue? The blue part of the election map? The Democrats?

Gravel-blind? And two types of apple? This makes no sense. Smashing? Ragnarok? The end of time?

What? The signs come down in flames? Like the pea sign or bean sign or whatever it was? Erasure of agents' names? The buried? The road get taken down? Shit—he is singing about us? "He can't do that," said Nan out loud.

"We're no James Gang," said Nin.

"Listen—what the fuck? He's trying to incite people against us! He wants a lynching!"

"Death to us? Wait—which one's the infidel? Which is god-fearing?"

"Oh, jeez. What are we going to do?"

"Ignore it."

"*Ignore* it? He's going to spread this song around until even the police like it."

"Oh—I remember reading an interview with Mark Mothersbaugh of *Devo*, and he said the scariest thing was that, when Devo was arrested for obscenity, the cops in the jailhouse started a conga line and removed their belts and snapped them in a dance circle to the CD of 'Whip It.' And they sang along, knowing all the words!"

"Maybe that's why he quit Devo and began writing music for *Rugrats* and other cartoons."

"Maybe," said Nin. "I still don't know if I get it all, even with the lyrics right here. The gibberish is beginning to sound like the Beatles' fake Italian in 'Sun King.'"

"Fake Italian or Kobaian?"

"Oh, shut up. Let me think."

"Okay."

They fell silent and went to opposite corners of the room and looked out the nearest window, as if in meditation. The truth was that they both had the dickens scared out of them. Of course, I'm scared of Dickens, too. Horribly out-of-date social satire aimed at targets long since dead. And with Dickens' being paid by the word, by the installment, one could smell something afoul in the air.

"*Snap swing* is definitely a lynching. We've got to stop him."

"Oh, that's easy," said Nan. "Where did he go?"

"Well, I'd say he went on down road, but—"

"There isn't any road! We tore it up, remember?"

"Okay, so we just follow his direction."

"Did you see the direction he left in?"

"No. We were busy arguing over petty shit."

"Well, I didn't either. And we have no idea the direction he came from."

"I'd guess from the urban sprawl."

"Well, that would make sense. So, he's heading into the wilderness? That makes no sense, because he has to spread his song."

"He could do that on-line. He could have his own internet radio station dedicated to hating us. They could be building an army against us!"

"Calm down! They can't do any of that until Brother Sam gets here. We have to figure out where he went. Or where he came from."

"Wait! We're assuming that he came from a place other than were he is going. What if this was not a stopover? What if it was the destination? He was on reconnaissance."

"No. I don't think so. That guy was a leader of nothing. Even his bullshit was fake. That's it! A guy who bought dozens of novelty gag gifts to spring on his friends EVERY DAY! But that's a different subject. What were we talking about?"

"I don't know."

"How to catch him. How to corner him and collect him."

"Come now—he is human, after all," said Nin.

"*Is* he?"

"You're not back on your Kobaian thing again, are you?"

"No. No. No. Sorry," replied Nan.

Nin returned to the center of the room. "If you're right, then Brother Sam might just have come from the nearest city over the hill and returned there!"

"I think that must be, Nin."

"Well, Nin, let's go"

"Should we bring umbrellas?"

Chapter Six: Finding Brother Sam

As soon as they saw a road, Nan broke down. Going on was inconceivable, so they stopped at the closest motel, the Stampeded Antelope.

"Your foot, it needs reinflation," said Nin. They'd been arguing about whether to walk or use the golf cart.

"Yeah, but I rolled," replied Nan, as if that were the answer. Well. Maybe it *is* the answer. What do I know?

Nan rowed while Nin looked at a map.

"What's up there?" asked Nan, pointing to a spot on the map.

"North," replied Nin.

Up the side of a rocky cliff, alongside mountain goats and big horn sheep, stood the Stampeded Antelope.

Naturally, therefore, the motel was decorated with a pirate motif. Rudders, nets, crabs, steering wheels and harpoons festooned the walls.

A coat of arms featured an oar at the fess point of an escutcheon.

Paintings of large vessels were hung in each room. Nin and Nan's room featured a frigate incongruously named *The Estancia*. One assumed she had transported cattle.

"Arrrr...," said Nan, in the best possible pirate accent that could be mustered. "They must have been pirate cattle. Arrrr..."

Why pirates? Who knew? The nearest navigable body of water was the Big River, some 200 miles away. As far as Nin knew, pirates had never broached it.

The lobby sported another incongruity—a loaded and

ready freewheeling trebuchet, pointed at the front door in case of a Viking incursion, perhaps.

The motel restaurant was called Captain Snagglebeard's, and Nin and Nan ordered "all-u-can-eat" clam strips from the limited menu.

Nan asked the one-eyed waiter if the restaurant carried HoJo cola, but the waiter stared back blankly and shook his head.

"Ow!" said Nan. "Stop shaking my head!"

"Arrr...," said the waiter, "then don't ask impertinent questions, if ye know what's good for ya."

After the waiter left. Nan asked Nin, "Who are Ye and Ya? Are they cousins of ours?"

"Shut up, will you? Drink your grog."

The atmosphere of the restaurant began changing later in the evening, and the waiters began leading the dining patrons in a sea chanty sing-along and, as Nan called it, Okefenokee Karaoke.

"Our ship, it sails at morning tide—
I signed aboard to leave my bride.
I'd met her when the night was young
and so was she, but not for long.
I went to bed aged 24
but woke up with a toothless whore.
Ten thousand pints can't wash away
what happened to me on that day.
Ten thousand knots I now must sail
Before I forget that harpooned whale..."

And so forth. Very uncomfortably sexist. Mindless. Of course. He could never mind his manners.

He starts the lawnmower. Now, briefly, he is alone. Then he turns, and you see him. You turn also.

He exceeds the posted speed limit for Buckhorn. 99¢ a 6-pack. And that's just the fine. Old way is different from the new way.

Older is newer.

Only squares get around.

"Our names? Oh, sorry. We are, as you know, Late Night Traditions."

"What the hell are you talking about?"

"Oh—I was just talking."

"No. You were dreaming," said Nin, propping up Nan.

"'I Have a Dream,'" laughed the collapsible one.

"Okay, over here. Just lie down in bed. Sleep it off." Nin unceremoniously stepped away from being Nan's crutch, and Nan crumpled onto the bed and was out cold. *Good thing's Nan's not face down*, thought Nin. *Nan can't die like Hendrix*.

Nin turned on the TV with the remote. The only TV in the room. Obviously... No.

Fellini's *Clowns* was on. Ah, the unbearable sadness of the clowns who used to be in the late great European circuses! They'd all been out of work for thirty years and still were sad. What a film!

Nin pulled a beer out of the microfridge and nuked some popcorn and began watching just in time to see the closing credits' being interrupted by a station promo for a new sitcom featuring an unsuccessful gas attendant who smokes around the pumps. It's not a question of *if* he'll kill himself, but *when*. Following Monday Night Football. Then a commercial for vaginal cream. I wonder why the station wants us to link those two messages. Then an Army recruitment ad. What's the LCD? "Have a ball"?

Nin switched channels and got sucked into the episode of *Monk* that consisted mostly of flashbacks to middle school, when Adrian was stuffed into his locker by a bully.

A cognac from Nin's suitcase and a copy of Kenneth Patchen's *Sleepers Awake* were all Nin needed to begin taking repose.

Nin lay down and started in on his Durante. He caught a big one but was too lazy to get up, so he buried it in his shirt.

Nan was snoring in the other bed. Nin realized that Nan was now face-up. Rolling Nan over again was hell—but Hendrix...

Nan needed a diet. Now!

Nan stopped snoring. Nin remembered a story on NPR about how each year hundreds of college students at party schools choke to death on their own vomit.

Nin personally had clung to toilet bowls and "let his face slide down the cool, smooth tile" like Jim Morrison.

They'd been unable to find out anything at Captain Snagglebeard's.

In the morning, Nan stumbled to the toilet, hung over, and threw up. Nin quickly exited to the hall and almost collided with a man wearing a pink bandana. He turned around and had a pink beard.

"Arrr... I'm Pinkbeard the Pirate" does not instill fear.

Nin laughed and walked on. This hotel spares no gag.

"Hurry," said Pinkbeard. "You'll miss him!"

"Who?"

"He's speaking in the conference room!"

"Who?"

"It's the first time he's ever been here!"

"*Who*?"

"Who? Why, Emperor Pinocchibush, of course!"

"That guy with the big donkey ears? Why's he here?"

"Where have you been? This is all newly annexed terri-tory, you landlubber. You are inside the empire."

"Oh, jeez."

Nin stopped and let Pinkbeard hurry on. Oh, no—Nin and Nan were not just criminals—they were criminals in-side Pinocchibush's empire. Pinocchibush the Ruthless. Pinocchibush the Patsy. Pinocchibush the Wooden Head-ed. Pinocchibush the Liar. He had a thousand faces and a thousand names.

The hotel bar was open, so Nin popped in for a shot and beer before facing the Oily One. A greased pig.

Into the crowd, let's be herded.

Politicians all herd their constituents.

There he is, straw hat, barefoot, chewing on dried grass.

"Yew people of the heartland are the heart of the Em-pire Pinocchibush," he was saying. Nin could have sworn Pinocchibush's nose had just grown.

"We have liberated you from yourselves. Now you will fashion yourselves in our image."

Sounds like the royal "we," thought Nin.

"Bull crap!" comes a yell from a few feet back in the crowd. "You liberated us from our oil! You eat while we starve!"

The outburst was quickly subdued by the Emperor's Secret Service, the notorious ESS.

"That young man is an example of the sort of dissent a free culture cannot tolerate," said the Emperor. "His lies—" at this point his nose grew again "—are anathema to an athematic society." What?

"Your Highness?" yelled a reporter from the front rows. "Would you tell us about your new nose?"

"What nose?" He looked cross-eyed at his nose, but stopped abruptly and said, "My nose is as it always is. Are you mocking your Emperor?" And the reporter was removed by ESS.

People began whispering. His nose! It grows when he lies, like that Italian puppeteer's little masterpiece. Ah, but he can't see it! The Emperor's New Nose!

The joke spread like free beer, and soon everyone was laughing at the Emperor. He got red as a Texas chili pepper and exploded. No—that wasn't him—that was a gunshot!

Nan woke up again later. Nin? Where was Nin? Obviously, there'd been a struggle—furniture was overturned, and the bathroom smelled like the scene of a crime [Nan, of course, did not remember tripping over the furniture in the mad rush to the toilet].

Nan came to the inexorable conclusion that Nin had been forcibly removed. The lack of blood suggested kidnapping.

Nan took the Mauser from the suitcase. Loaded it. Put it in a shoulder holster, strapped the shoulder holster on, put a windbreaker over it—the windbreaker was blue and cotton-lined and had a red C in a blue circle, signifying the Chicago Cubs.

When Nan found Nin carrying on in the company of the enemy, thoughts of betrayal took over.

No—the room was not overturned in a struggle! Nin had arranged it to look that way. Nin was selling them out for thirty pieces of silver. To save Nin's own ass, Nin had betrayed them. Nin would get off easy for collaborating. Nan would fry. Oh, that's how it's going to be, is it? No way. I can't permit that.

Nan rushed towards Nin, pulled out the Mauser, pointed it at Nin and fired while tripping over some idiot's stupid feet.

The bullet lodged itself in the Emperor's ample behind. Before Nan could think, an insanely motivated Nin leapt up from the orchestra seats and landed at Nan's side, spun Nan around and pushed Nan through an exit into a waiting cab at a speed too fast for even to ESS to react to.

"For the border," said Nin. The cabbie turned around. For a second Nin thought the cabbie was Brother Sam—from behind the hair was similar. Thank goodness it wasn't. Or, rather, curses that it hadn't been!

Nan said, "This is great, just great! Now they're probably after us for attempted ass—"

"Shh!" Nin said, clapping a hand over Nan's mouth. "Taximeter cabriolets have auditory capabilities."

"And you! You were about to betray us!"

"No—not in a million years."

"But you were up there."

"Just an innocent spectator. I was carried there by the throng of the crowd."

"I thought—I was going to—"

"Shoot me? Ha ha! You've never been able to hit the side of a farm."

"A barn."

"That, too," laughs Nin. "You'd never have hurt me. It was all an accident."

"But—"

"It was all an *accident*. Now, drop it. We have to find Brother Uncle Sam."

"Excuse me!" the cabbie interjected. "You're lookin' for Uncle Sam the musician?"

"Yep."

"You're in luck. Look over there." The marquee at the Dune Beetle Lounge announced "One Night Only—In His Last Officially Permitted Concert—Uncle Sam Slammassa-soit!" Apparently, the Emperor was not going to tolerate American propaganda.

"Quick!" yelled Nin, throwing a couple of bills at the cabbie. "Here we are!"

The thick, putrid aroma of thick, putrid people came pummeling all who approached, compounded by a pounding that could loosen fire hydrants from their moorings.

On stage, Uncle Sam, solo acoustic again, was cater-wauling some inhuman sex song. The audience was grunting in unison.

Nan didn't want another explosion, but Nin pushed.

When the god-awful noise ended, Nin rushed up to Sam, pulled his hair down towards his shoulders for attention, and said in his ear, "You will not play that song."

"What? What song?"

"Don't give me that. *The Nin and Nan Song*, you perv."

"No—not a perv. Just an opportunist. But Pinocchibush is shutting me down anyway."

"Have you done the song?"

Nan came up, too. "Yeah, have you done the song yet?"

"Sure—a couple of places before I visited you."

"Here?"

"No."

"You're lucky."

"Hey, I hate that pig Pinocchibush as much as you do. I'll tell you what—I'll lose that song forever if you can help me get artists' rights reestablished in this country. The media's been bought out by the Emperor, and the artists dominating all the charts are plants."

"What?" asked Nan. "Venus Flytraps?"

"No, goofball," said Nin. "Like government spies."

"Like revenuers?"

"Exactly like revenuers."

"Then Old Brother Sam here isn't a revenuer?"

Sam started laughing. "Me? A revenuer? That'd be the day. I spit on revenuers."

Nan looked confused. "But the song..."

"A tribute, man," replied Sam. "I heard about what you two were doing from some old sheep herder, and I thought it was cool. So I wrote the song. It's sarcastic."

That shook Nan's head. "Oh, boy," was all Nan could say.

"Cabbie!" yelled Nin once they were outside, pointing at one.

"Don't do that—I have a van. Here—help me load my equipment and I'll drive."

"Drive where?" asked Nan.

"I'm assuming you want me to help you find the shepherd."

"Excellent. Let's go, Brother!" said Nin.

Chapter Seven: The Way of the Shepherd

Shall not the way of the shepherd be but a tree in the ocean? A lone shepherd, flock before him, stands on a hillside and sees something interesting.

Who's he going to tell? The sheep? His dog?

Oh, I see—a well-placed rocket grenade and even his dog won't be able to tell anyone anything.

Maybe he can be reasoned with. Unlikely, but I should never overlook that possibility.

They stopped at a diner for dinner.

Sam lifted his knife from his Salisbury steak and gestured with it. "The shepherd could be anywhere in a twenty-mile radius, I figure," he said.

"Oh, spare me," said Nin at the same instant that Sam's grand gesture signifying a twenty-mile square led his hand into contact with Nan's nose. The knife scratched Nan's cheek.

"Ow!" said Nan. "I said, 'spare me,' not 'spear me,' you clod!"

"Well, at least you get my point," said Sam."

"Let me look at that," said Nin, examining the cut. "Oh, that's not even deep enough to rub salt into for a good fencing scar. Now, come one. Listen to Brother Sam."

"Well, when I met him," said Sam, "he said he'd just come from the eastern edge of his sheep's run, where the large pond over by you is."

"It's a small lake," said Nin, "and it only touches on the edge of our area."

"Whatever. That's where he saw you. And he's old, so

he's not going to graze his sheep over an endless expanse."

"Okay."

"And everyone knows that shepherds graze the sheep between a water hole at one end and a salt lick at the other—"

"So all we have to do," interrupted Nin, "is find where the nearest salt lick is, and we can define the grazing grounds!"

"I think that's how that works."

"I hope you're right," said Nan.

"Oh, ye of little faith," said Nin. "Trust me. We'll find him."

Nan looked out the window at the parking lot. A salmon Stingray was at one end and a white Pathfinder at the other. The street signs identified the restaurant as located on Morton Street between Pickles and Lam. A blue Barracuda was cruising the lot. Abruptly, the driver switched the Barracuda into reverse and backed into a stall without ever looking behind. Unfortunately a refried-bean-colored Pinto was already in that stall and exploded when the Barracuda slammed into its infamous and exposed rear-mounted gas tank. Refried-bean-colored crap blew all over the place. Someone with overalls and firefighter boots showed up with a shovel to clean up the mess.

"Nan!" Nan became conscious of the fact that Nin had been saying 'Nan!' for a few minutes. Seconds?

"What?" snapped Nan, not wanting to lose the reverie.

"Nothing. The waiter wants to know if you want another beer. Duh."

Nan looked up. Sure enough, the waiter was standing there expectantly.

"Bring me a Colt 45," snarled Nan, remembering a movie title: *They Shoot Horses, Don't They?* When the 24-ounce can arrived at the table, Nan asked to borrow the waiter's pen.

Nan turned the beer upside down and slammed the pen tip through the bottom of the can, puncturing a neat round hole in it. Nan began sucking the beer out of the hole while turning the can rightside up and popping the top. The entire contents of the 24-ounce beer flew down Nan's gullet so fast that a bunch of it came out through Nan's nose. Nan's eyes watered, but, shaking it off, Nan snorted and said, "Now, what were you saying, Nin?"

"Sam was saying that the old shepherd's a crook," said Nin, which was enough for Nan, whose instant guffaw brought all the beer back up over the table.

Nin got up and got some bar rags and threw them at Nan. "Here, pig. Clean up your mess." And Nin and Sam changed tables.

The Emperor came on the television and began to speak:

"I'd like to respond to the recent outbursts that occurred at my appearance at the Stampeded Antelope resort. Those responsible will be brought to justice and, I swear, will not be misapprehended. Those who resort thus are declared enemies of the state, and their deeds will not go unattended. They will be tried, true, and convicted upon sentencing to corporal punishment of the worst kind when we find them. Let this be a lesson to those who would defrock their Emperor! Thus have I spaken!"

"Holy crap. Did he just declare tourist resorts illegal?" asked Sam. Nan wiped up the beer at the next table.

"I don't know what the hell he said," replied Nin, shrugging. "Does *he* even know?"

"No—he just tried to read those cue cards."

"Well, I hope he gives his son some acting lessons. We can't have an Emperor acting like this."

"No," chuckled Sam. "We can't. Maybe, after we find the shepherd, we could do something to help." He winked at Nin.

"Yeah. Maybe."

While wiping the next table, Nin noticed a fellow at the table on the other side of Nin and Sam paying undue attention to the conversation. "Nin. Sam. Shh! Taximeter cabriolets have auditory capabilities," Nan said.

Sam and Nin turned and looked at the man, who immediately hid behind a menu.

"All I know," said Sam, "is that anyone eavesdropping will be sorry."

"That's for sure," rejoindered Nin. The man buried himself even deeper in the menu. "An eavesdropper is like a peeping Tom. And you know what happens to them."

"The Emperor's dungeon, if he's lucky. But I heard they're usually beaten to death on the way." The waiter went to the man's table.

"They're stoned by the crowd lining the streets to the dungeon." The man asked if the restaurant served squab.

"Unless they're maimed for life by those they've wronged, who, of course, get the first shot." The waiter shook his head. The man, feigning indignation, stood up, turned and hurried out of the restaurant.

"I guess the restaurant doesn't serve stool pigeons," said Sam, laughing.

"Or any other kind," said Nin, laughing along. Nan, finished with the wiping, tossed the rag onto the table and rejoined the two.

"Now, that wasn't necessary," said Nan, grinning.

"*Au contraire*," said Nin. "*Au contraire*."

"Well, we'd better move along," said Sam, "in case that was someone." They dropped a tip onto the table and went out into the parking lot just in time to see their neighbor speed off in a cream-colored Dodge Ram.

"After him?" asked Nan.

"No. We don't have the time," said Nin.

"Guys," said Sam. "I just remembered where I'd seen that guy. He seemed so familiar. And younger. But I'm pretty sure, without his wild white hair and long beard, that was our shepherd. He's gone incognito. He knows we're onto him! Quick! Into the Batmobile!"

"I thought it was a three-quarter ton Bonaventure."

"Okay. The Samobile!"

"Yeah."

By the time they were all settled into their seatbelts, the Ram was long gone.

"Nin?"

"Yes, Nan?"

"Did you see the direction he left in?"

"No. We were busy buckling up."

"No problem, gang," said Sam. "It's all one-ways from

here. He could have only gone one way." Nin noticed the construction detour signs ahead.

"Too bad we don't have something that corners," said Nan.

"Hold on," said Sam, flooring the accelerator. The afterburners kicked in as the van switched to turbo. It lifted up onto its two hind wheels and took off.

"If he's hungry, he's going to be stopping at a restaurant soon," said Nan. "Did he stop to eat, or to spy on us?" asked Nin.

"I think that must have been a coincidence," said Sam. "And when he saw me with you, he must have assumed that the song was my using him for a chump."

"So he's figuring you gave him the song to distract him while you collected us for the bounty," said Nan.

"Otherwise he would have known the bounty is on all our heads and would have tried to collect us himself," said Sam.

"He's too little to get all three of us," said Sam.

"Not if he had his pals Smith and Wesson with him," replied Sam.

"So we can assume he's not out to collect us," said Nin.

"True," replied Sam. But he might sell us out to the highest bidder."

"Crud! How did we get into this in the first place? Nin, it's all your fault. Opening doors to strangers. What were you thinking?"

"Actually, I did us a favor. The shepherd had already seen us, remember? He could have gone to turn us in and we'd never have known until the ATF showed up."

"True."

"You can kiss my feet now in gratitude."

"Not until you've been defeated," said Nan.

"Then you're going to have a long wait," replied Nin, "because we're not going to lose."

"Up here is another restaurant. Cruise the parking lot. Look for the Ram," ordered Sam.

They came upon the Crow Bar cautiously. The parking lot and an automobile wrecker stood side-by-side with a barbed-wire fence separating them, and one couldn't tell the cars belonging to one from those belonging to the other. Sam thought he spotted a Ram inside the wrecker's yard and said the wrecker might be in cahoots with the shepherd.

When they walked into the place, the entire joint was watching the TV and singing along the "My Beloved Emperor," the song preceding all ball games and Emperor's Addresses.

The patrons looked like mostly employees from next door: automotive coveralls were *de rigueur*. Some of them had to dry their eyes after declaring their fealty. A royalist crowd, to say the least.

The speech began:

"My citizens," began the Emperor, nose neat and trimmed short. "I stand before you because we cannot stand for any terrorist activity in our land."

"Yeah, and because you can't sit," laughed Nin.

"The terrorists need to resort their priorities and should only uphold the sort that is not traitorous."

"Huh? Oh, make him stop already, Nin."

Nin & Nan

"Shh!" Sam whispered. "Royalists! Sit here!" He sat down and abruptly pulled Nin and Nan down into a booth facing the giant screen face of Pinocchibush. "Copy their movements!"

When the patrons dropped to their knees, so did Nin, Nan and Sam. When the patrons swooned, so did Nin, Nan and Sam. When the patrons cheered, so did Nin, Nan and Sam. Well, maybe not Nan, who instinctively suspected any synchronized activity. But, even without being fully convinced, even Nan played along.

The speech droned on. "And so henceforth we shall seek death for all international terriers that try to get in our way!"

A couple of dog owners got up and hurried out of the place.

"Only terriers?" asked a reporter.

"Them and all those beasts that support them."

A few more pet owners got up, and among them was the shepherd. He hadn't noticed Nin, Nan and Sam.

What was really unfortunate was that this was the very weekend the World Terrier Championships were being held in the city. Dogs all over the place started acting strange. The terriers were being hunted. Sometimes packs of mongrels would turn them in.

The Emperor's popularity ebbed, especially in the new territory, but one would never have known that in the Crow Bar. Heck, that crappy Bruce Springsteen song "Born in the USA" was even playing on the jukebox.

"The Way of US or the Way of None!" read a biker's bottomrocker.

"Um, Nin?"

"Yes, Nan?"

"Did you see the direction he left in?"

"Don't worry. If he's hungry, he's going to be stopping at a restaurant soon," said Nin.

"That's right!" said Nan, relieved.

Chapter Eight: The 3rd Restaurant, the 3rd TV

"The Third Eye. I've been visited by something that doesn't want me to succeed."

"That's ridiculous, Nan," said Nin. "Superstitious hog-wash."

"Like you'd know."

"Stop it, you two," intervened Sam. "It's bad when I have to be the mature one here. I'm a musician, damn it!"

"Wait! There's a flaw in the ointment!" interjected Nan.

"Meaning a fly?" interpreted Nin.

"Cut it out, you two," intercepted Sam. "I mean it. Or I'll have to intra-duce you two to my two dukes," he said, holding up a suspiciously-not-so-frail-looking pair of fists.

At this rate, by the time dinner's over, we'll have been to a dozen restaurants and Sam will be as large as

a bounty hunter? thought Nan.

or worse, thought Nin.

What's worse?

A stooge for the machine.

"And what evidence have ye?"

"Empirical, of course."

"Hey, guys," said Sam. "I know her," pointing to a corner table inside the Third Eye.

"That's a table, Sam."

"No—the woman who was sitting there a minute ago."

"Who?"

"You didn't notice her?"

"Not really, Sam. I'm not here to score with the Chicks

Eckhard Gerdes

"Don't worry. We got him. This time I got his distributor cap."

"If you had the right car."

"Of course I had the right car! Who do you take me for? A Pinocchibushy?"

"Okay. So he's here somewhere. This is a huge place."

"Well, duh. It's a casino."

They walked past an old patron at a slot machine who was so heavy into her addiction that she'd forgotten herself and had soiled her pants. Badly. One employee walked over to help, but a manager stopped him. "Not until she's finished betting, son. Then you can go get a mop and bucket since you want to be so 'helpful.'" And thank her for coming to Pinocchibushoil Casino, "where every handshake is greezy!"

They walked over to a roulette wheel looking for shoeblack.

The crap tables stank. Madam Comnist walked over to Sam, whispered in his ear, and took off.

"What was that?" asked Nan.

"Nothing. I couldn't even understand her. Nin, do you have a pen?"

"We're staying?"

"Let me just say I think I got us a room."

"Sam, you're okay," said Nin.

"We'll see," said Nan. Muttering.

"What?"

"Nothing. Sounds great." For you. I'll be left without a friend.

"Beth, here, will be your friend tonight, Nan."

"Cool. Hey, Beth. What's your favorite rock and roll band?"

"Ew. Maybe, oh, the Beatles!"

"Good answer. Okay. Now we've got something to talk about!"

Nin and Nan went up to the room, 369, just as they had said they would. And the room was open just as Beth had said. Unfortunately, Beth wasn't in it. That was sarcastic. Beth had to score some crank. But she had a room. And room service! Neither champagne nor caviar was too good for Beth!

"Get the Dom Perignon and make sure that's 100% Caspian Sea black sturgeon caviar."

"You got it! Thanks, Beth! Wherever you are! Hey, aren't we supposed to be looking for the shepherd?"

"No. That's Sam's job. We're just supposed to get drunk and pass out."

"Oh," and they did. The TV woke them. It came on automatically at 3:30 a.m. to share an urgent message from His Highness.

"But first a word from our sponsor, Makil Health Care. Now that Asian Bird Flu has been found in poultry in Turkey, protect yourself with a Makil flu shot. Payable in easy monthly installments of $29.95!"

"How did the poultry get eaten by turkeys?" asked Nan. "Are turkeys cannibalistic?"

"I don't know. Shh! Our illustrious leader is about to speak."

"Nothing up my sleeve. Presto!"

"Shush!"

"Maybe it's just the sick ones. Like those mad cows that were going around eating sheep."

"Don't tell that to the shepherd until we've caught him."

"Maybe we should disguise ourselves as a mad cow!"

"Oh, hush. Listen."

"And now! Live from the Empire City, His Highness!" Canned applause.

"Good evening, My Subjects. I have been told by my advisors that some of you have tried and failed and have deconstrued incorrectly what my earlier states meant, er, statements, er, meant. If you have assumed I have leveled a permanent ban on resorts and terriers, you have misapprehended me incorrectly. Though we need to guard against terriers' activities in our resorts, I of course am not suggesting we close our hostilitality industries. But let me not allay your fears one more second—every dog has his day.

"Now is not the time to take the streets in protest—"

Nin and Nan exchanged a glance. *We* took a street.

"Now is the time to reclaim the streets in the name of the Empire. Streetwashers, stop washing. Streetwalkers, stop walking. Give back what has always belonged to the people. The streets, sidewalks, and the gutter.

"Thus have I spaken!"

Man, though Nin. He just condemned the commoner to the gutter. If *that* doesn't stir them up, what will?

And the station broadcast the Makil Health Care advertisement again. People walking down the street, albatrosses on their backs, turn into the Makil Health Care Center, then come out a revolving door, sans albatross. Wait! One of those people! It's the shepherd. He goes in, but he never comes out. He didn't have an albatross on his back. Almost as if he'd just coincidentally decided to enter the building there just then. Of course, accidents don't exist, chaos doesn't exist. William Burroughs said that if you ever think chaos exists, look to see if anyone's profiting by it. Sure enough, someone will be, and you'll realize that chaos does not really exist. Nan was lost in thought.

"Did you see that?" asked Sam.

"That was the shepherd?"

"I think so."

"Nan? Did you see it?"

"Huh? What?"

"The shepherd going into that building."

"What? Oh, the shepherd. Where?"

"That was the Makil Health Care Center."

"Graceless," said Nan.

"Gracious," corrected Nin. Nan scowled.

"Graceless," repeated Nan, with emphasis.

"That's the first target, kids," said Sam.

"We're short, not young," replied Nan indignantly.

"It's designed as a huge cross, each wing dedicated to one speciality: hysterectomy, tonsillectomy, circumcision, and cosmetic surgery."

"How do you know that?"

"TV commercials, Holmes. Like everyone else."

"Which one do you think our shepherd would be involved with, do you suppose?"

"I suppose stockings. I don't know. What does he prefer: playing with his mouth, playing with his pud, playing with his neighbor's toys, or conceptualizing bodily perfection?"

Tough question. I don't even know if I could tell you for myself, even less for someone else.

Yes, that's me! "Even Less For Someone Else." Nin looked at Nan, who was falling asleep. I hope Beth has a sense of humor. Better order some more Dommy P. before she gets back. She's not likely to order it herself. Oh, well. She thought Nan was cute and I was clever. Madam Comnist knew them. From years ago. We don't talk about it. It's over and done with. It's in the pond in the park, and ducks down to use it.

Ducks drown to use it.

Chapter Nine: The Makil Health Care Center

"Of or pertaining to the uterus" is the definition of "hysteria." Thus, to cure women [note: *only* women exhibit hysteria, by definition] of their hysteria, doctors rip out their uteruses.

Whenever a typical doctor treats a woman and cannot figure out what is truly wrong with her, that doctor dismisses it as "hysteria" and cuts out her uterus.

Of course, the doctors caught on to the fact that the jig was up about the word "hysteria" and changed their prognosis to "premenstrual syndrome" and came up with expensive placebos to cure the imaginary ailment, or rather the single ailment that included thousands of unrelated symptoms.

Take these pills, Alice. They'll cure you. How dare you stand there and bleed all over the place?

I remember my insurance paperwork once stating, "Pregnancy will be treated like any other illness," i.e. as a disease only doctors know how to cure. Before doctors, women could not be cured of their pregnancies.

A man was arguing with a nurse at a nurse's station. His gestures were violent, his pointing finger a dagger in the air.

"My wife loved me before she came in here for this completely unnecessary operation, and now she won't have anything to do with me," he was saying. "And it's *your* fault."

"Sir, I wasn't even on duty that day."

"Not *you*. All of you. You greedy slimebags who'd rip

out a woman's innards in exchange for memberships at the exclusive 'no-women, no-Blacks, no-Jews' country clubs. You hate women so much you can't even stand to have their innard-less bodies on your links. That's it, isn't it?"

"Sir, I wasn't there. And I don't golf."

"Of course not. They don't allow you to."

"Who?"

"The doctors. The greedy scum who cut out my wife's love for me."

"Sir, I'll get you a supervisor. Just a minute."

Nin watched her mouth the word "security" into the phone. Nin walked up to the man.

"Hey, man. I agree with you, but you'd better get the hell out of here. She just called security, and the rentacops will be here to rough you up in just a minute."

"They cut up my wife—"

"I know. And they'll cut you up, too. I think they're still conducting Mengele's phosphorous experiments on the behavior ward patients."

"What?"

"No joke, man. Go!"

"Thanks," and he ran. Nin saw him wave from his car in the parking lot just as the rentacops showed up.

"A friend of yours?" asked one of the steroidal rentacops.

"No—not at all. I was only telling him what the time was. I'm here to see a friend. A shepherd friend of mine who until recently had a beard checked in, and I want to visit him. Where's his room?"

"How should I know?" asked the rentacop.

True, thought Nin. Steroids have rotted your brain. You are way too stupid to be qualified for anything other than being a rentacop or a politician. At least two regions had, within, recent memory, "elected" (such a term could only be used lightly inside the Empire) steroid-befuddled former pseudo-athletes as their governors. Several others had hired empty-shelled actors to play the parts of their representatives. The worst, though, were incapable of discerning between ministers and "ministers of state," so they gave over their governance to whatever religious organizations had their boys by the balls.

Sam derailed this train of thought. "Excuse me, my good man," he said to the friggin' rentacop. It was embarrassing, conciliatory, submissive. A sort of Stepin' Fetchit routine. "I also am a friend of the shepherd. Whom may I make my inquiry of regarding his room location?"

The rentacop's head spun around three times and then exploded.

Another rentacop came over. "Model J42 just exploded. We need a replacement." Presumably he was communicating with someone.

The nurse said, "I just looked up our admissions. He's not here. Of course, this is mostly a women's ward. Have you tried Circumcisions?"

"Why?" asked Nan. "Aren't there women admitted there?"

"No! Female circumcision? How barbaric!" said the nurse, seeming shocked.

"But male circumcision?"

"That's for good hygiene."

"Oh. You know, toes have more infections and hygiene problems than penises do. Why don't you just lop off everyone's toes?"

"They might over in cosmetic surgery. I'm not sure. You'd have to check over there."

"Okay. Come on, Nan. Sam, come on. We've got to go to the circumcision ward."

"Why would our shepherd want a circumcision?" asked Nan.

"Who knows? Maybe he heard the voice of God," said Nin.

"And so he wants to cut off the head of God?" asked Nan.

"I have an idea," said Sam. "But we're going to need to find the hub of this place."

"Hub?"

"Yeah, you know. The physical plant. The communications center. The hub of the nexus."

"Here's the next ward. Ask the nurse."

"Excuse me. Where's your physical plant?"

"Mnnnbrngrnrbrngr..."

"What?" Nin and Nan exchanged confused glances.

"Oh," said Nin. "This is the tonsillectomy ward. They're pulling *everyone*'s tonsils out, apparently. Even the nurses'."

"We'd better keep going. I need my tonsils. They protect me against infection," said Sam.

"Look—a poster for a bargain. Today only—they're doing free appendectomies with every tonsillectomy sold," said Nan, feigning excitement.

"As I said, we'd better keep going. I'm led to believe that stepping onto the hospital grounds is implied consent for experimental treatment."

"Here's a sign that says, 'no admittance.' This must be it," said Nin. "Here we go." Nin and Nan followed Sam into the communications center. He whispered something to the operator, who scurried away like a cockroach. Sam picked up the hospital's P.A. system microphone and switched the "all on" button.

"Attention, all hospital patrons. This is God. And I'm looking for the shepherd whose beard was recently shaven."

Sam covered the microphone with his hands. "You go out to the entrances and catch him if he tries to leave," said Sam. Nin and Nan hurried out. "I am your God, and I want you to prepare a sacrifice. Bring your son to the altar and sacrifice him to me." Sam was betting the shepherd had a son whom he had left in charge of the flock. "Should you so much as question my demand, and I shall smite all your descendents throughout all of eternity."

The shepherd, looking up at the loudspeaker, under-stood. However, he had no son. That he remembered. He sped out of the hospital, sheath intact, and hurried into the arms of Nin and Nan.

"Wait a minute, shepherd," said Nin. "Where are you hurrying off to?"

"I have to find my son."

"Oh, and where is your son?"

"I don't know." Just then Sam joined them.

"Hey, you, singer—I know you."

"Hello, old shepherd. Where are you off to?"

"To find my son, but I don't know where to find him."

Nan began to say, "Leave him alone and he'll come home," but Nin elbowed Nan's ribs hard.

"Ow!"

Sam winked at Nan and Nin. "Hey, we were just talking about how we needed an adventure. How about my friends and I help you find him?"

"Really? I'd be grateful."

"Of course." Sam whispered into Nan's ear,

"We'll be able to keep a close eye on him now, at least."

Nin was thinking they'd take a long walk down a short beer.

Chapter Ten: The Happy Hunting Grounds

"I had a wallet made of foreskins. Whenever I rubbed it, it turned into a briefcase," said Sam.

"That joke is as old as the heels," said Nin.

"So's that metaphor," said Nin.

"Do not mock the Lord," said the shepherd.

"Man, you sound like Nan," said Nin.

"What's your name?" asked Nan.

"Said," said Said, the shepherd.

"Said?" asked Sam.

"Said," said Said.

"Said?"

"Said said, 'Said.'"

"Said said, 'Said'?"

"Said said, 'Said said, "Said,"'" said Sam chuckling.

Said said, "Said" again, for emphasis.

"That's your name?" asked Sam.

"Man, you sound like Nan," said Nin.

"Do not mock the Lord," said Said.

"And *that* saying predates the meteor that killed the dinosaurs," said Sam. "Want me to turn on the radio?"

"No," said Said, so Nan did. A woman was singing a song about society. Nan immediately was captivated by the timbre of her voice and the sloppy arhythmic drumming behind her.

"That drummer's as sloppy as Keith Moon," said Nan.

"So turn it off, then," said Nin.

"No. I love Keef Spoon."

"Nin, you should appreciate all kinds of music," said

Sam.

"Sheesh," said Nin and Said simultaneously.

"*Parescum paribus facillime congregantur*," said Sam.

"What?" asked Nan.

"Birds of a feather flake their feathers," said Sam.

"Oh," and the jingle announcing a speech by the Emperor came on.

"Not again."

Nin turned the radio off.

"No, leave it on," said Nan.

"Oh, god, it's awful."

"You gotta know what he's saying." Nan turned it on.

"The trade imbalance is impaired by terriers and bailiffs," said the Emperor.

Nin turned the radio off. "Be real. He doesn't make any sense anyway."

"Leave it on," said Nan, switching it on again.

"For the most part, the peoples stink the way I do," said the Emperor.

Then a well-timed ad for deodorant soap came on. Even Nin couldn't take it, as when even strengthening accord.

As when even strengthening accord, evening was more than we could afford. Through the telephone was broadcast the voice of irate Beth: ripped me off, Dom Perignon? You didn't even leave me a glassful. My Big Brother knows you're there.

"Sam, you idiot. You gave her your number?"

"It seemed like a good idea at the time."

"Famous last words. You've got to ditch that phone.

They have global positioning systems in them. Now that you called in for messages, they can find us."

"Do not fear her big brother," said the shepherd, flinging the phone out the window. "Only the Lord can see where we are and where we are going."

"I guess in the larger, philosophical sense, that's true," said Nan.

As when even strengthening accord, Nin kicked Ninself in the butt. They needed some of the rest of the saints. That'd recover their divinity. And even a cute angel has angles. A dowager turned to a dowitcher and said, "Fly me away over the firewater and set my keester on the kieselguhr." Nin turned awee.

"Stop that!" said Nan. "Your spinning's making me dizzy."

"Don't tell me. Tell Jenny."

"Beth," said Sam.

"Oh, play us a song on the spinneret," said Nin. "I'll see you all later." And Nin left.

"What's gotten into Nin?" asked Sam.

"Nin's not big on the radio," answered Nan.

"Bad ratings?" asked the shepherd.

"No. Not like that. Even God has bad ratings. Nin just doesn't like much popular music or talk radio."

"What does Nin like?"

"Old radio shows. *The Green Hornet*. *The Shadow*. *Inner Sanctum*. That kind of stuff."

"Politics today are the greatest radio play of all," said Sam.

"I don't think Nin thinks so," said Nan.

"Sure does. This is part of Nin's act in it."

"I do not think that Nan does not think that Nin thinks so," said Said. "For if Nan did, the Lord would think, So what? But he has not revealed that to me."

"The Lord would think? So what? What are you saying, man?" challenged Sam.

"We must be in a moon void-of-course."

"'We must be in a moon void, of course'?"

"Never mind."

"Nevermind? What? In Bloom?"

"Is that Joyce?"

"You mean Beth?"

Will you all just shut up? My house has just been invaded by ladybugs and box elder bugs—there go those elders chasing the young ladies again—and I can barely walk without crunching something. Even the harmless can be annoying. Unless annoyance is their harm.

They attack the paper I am writing on. They distract me from the table. Now I have nothing to Chase Manhattans down with the fascist regime! What am I hunting for, again? Meaning? Or just the next word? Or do I want the last word? Omega. Which ends in an alpha, which begins the whole stinkin' process all over again.

Similarly, the consonant alphabet ends on a vowel. What? Only one vowel ends on a consonant. I tell you, English ain't fair. Ignore that linguist behind the curtain. He's not really the Great Linguini!

"Poseur!" I want to hear you yell.

Help that shy manicotti come out of his shell, would ya?

Recording the events as they occurred is difficult when all the voices come at once.

"Nan? Wake up!" The writer crashed the cymbals like Mick Fleetwood in the *Blues Jam in Chicago.*

"He's no fun—he fell right over," said Sam, quoting Firesign Theatre.

And pop goes the weasel.

Ping! The arrow was loosed, and the weasel was killed, teeth locked on the eagle's jugular. And eagle-weasel stew fed them at the campsite that night.

Eager-Weasel Stu came upon them from the freight yard and asked if they would share their libation.

"If you mean this god-awful stew," said Sam, "be our guest."

"Do not blaspheme!" said Said.

"No, I mean what he's drinking when you're not looking," said Stu, pointing to Said's jacket pocket.

Sam reached in and pulled out a pint of rotgut. "Aha! Don't talk to me of blasphemy, old man. For all you know, this could be your son."

Said squinted at Stu, sized up his features, and said, "Are you of the covenant?"

"Huh?"

"Are you of the covenant?"

"What do you mean?"

"He means," explained Nan, "have you had a chunk of your penis lopped off by illiterate believers who don't understand what Paul meant in Galatians when he said the ritual had been 'abrogated.'"

"What Nan means," explained Sam, "is are you

circumcised?"

"What a rude question," answered Stu. "I only wanted a snort."

"My son was circumcised."

"Well, not that it's any of your business, but so was I."

"Aha!" said Said. "Tie Isaac to that rock. I must prepare the sacrifice."

"No, Said. Don't you have to take him to the top of the mountain first?" pointed out Sam, gesturing towards the top of the hill.

"Oh, yes. Well, Son. Well met. You will accompany us. You will be well fed and made ready for the Lord."

"Can I have a snort of that bottle?"

"Sure. Have it all. We'll get you more tomorrow."

"Thanks, Father."

Sam said as an aside to Nan, "I think we can assume Said believes in the God of the Old Testament, not the New."

"And you think they are different?" asked Nan.

"Well, at the very least, the Old Testament God was far more immature than the New Testament one."

"Ah, you've read Alfred North Whitehead."

"Who?"

"Forget it."

"Alfred Lord Penishead?"

"I said forget it. You're as bad as Nin."

"Speaking of whom," said Sam, raising his voice to include Said and Stu, "I wonder where the hell—"

Said raised his eyebrows.

"—where the heck Nin is. Then Sam reboarded his

previous train:

"Alfred White Skinhead?"

"Hush."

"Alfred Popped Blackheads?"

"Be quiet."

"Didn't he write *The Idiots of the King*?"

"*Idylls*, and that was Alfred Lord Tennisball, as Python said. Now please be quiet. You're giving me a migraine."

"I pain, you pain, we all pain for migraine."

"What a reet. No wonder your music career is shit."

"Hey!"

"Wait, young Nan," said Said. "You are unfair. Sam here has a brilliant ballad he once shared with me. I don't remember the words, but it was called 'Busy Buzzy' or something."

Nan rolled the eyes at Sam. "He doesn't remember the song?"

At the top of the hill, Said said again, "Now tie Isaac to the rock!"

Nan looked around. "What rock, Said?"

"Do not call me Said. My name of the covenant is Abraham."

Nan laughed. "I can't believe I'm up here with you three stooges."

Said tied up Stu with twine, pushed him down onto the ground, and then pulled out a long, serrated chef's knife. He lifted the knife and was about to bring it down. Then an 8000-watt amplified voice boomed across the hillside: "Abraham!" The voice was so loud, Nan's ears rang.

It repeated: "Abraham!"

"Yes, Lord!" said Said, trembling.

"Put down that knife!"

"Stupid knife! Ugly knife! Knife of the guttersnipe!" said Nan, laughing.

Sam slapped Nan's arm.

"What? The Lord said to put it down."

"Ha ha."

Said backed away from Stu and dropped the knife. "Lord?"

"I want you to leave here and get a job at a 7-11 and never say anything about this to anyone ever again!"

"Yes, Lord."

"And I want you to forget Sam's song."

"I don't remember it anyway."

"Oh, shit," said the Lord.

"The Lord just cussed," said Nan, elbowing Sam in the ribs. "Come on. Let's get out of here."

"What about Said and Stu?"

"Forget about them. It's over."

Down the hill, Sam and Nan got in the car, and Nin ran up and joined them.

"They really fell for that, didn't they?" said Nin, tossing a microphone and a small Pignose amp into the back of the van.

"Hey, you took my Pignose?"

"Borrowed. Not took."

"That was good. That was really good," said Nan.

"That should do it," agreed Sam.

"For Said and Stu. We still have Pinocchibush to worry about, though," said Nin. "But now, let's get a few drinks."

Chapter Eleven: Finding the Needle in a Hayseed

"No, the Emperor is many people. The true Emperor never appears in public. He has a series of doppelgängers appear for him, pretending to be him," said the bartender to Nin.

"The problem must be finding doppelgängers stupid enough," said Nan.

"Actually, that's not difficult. The plastic surgery required to duplicate them must be the most complicated part of the procedure," said Sam.

"Where's all this plastic surgery done, do you think?" asked Nin.

Nan and Sam looked at each other and answered simultaneously, "the Makil Health Care Center!"

"Yes. We need to go back there."

"To the cosmetic surgery wing?"

"Of course."

The receptionist looked at them as they approached the hospital's cosmetic surgery registration desk.

"May I help?" she asked with suspicion in her voice. Her gray hair was long, like a little girl's, but her face had given up childhood decades earlier. Her voice was raspy, like a lifelong, boozin', smokin' cabaret singer's. Sam half-expected her to burst into Brecht and Weill's "Alabama Song."

"What procedure are you here for?"

"Do you guys do toe-lop-off-to-me's?" asked Nan. "The penis mutilators said you might."

"No. If you're here to cause trouble, I'll just call security now," she said, reaching for the phone.

"No!" yelled Nin. "Excuse us. Nan here sometimes loses site of our objectives. Actually, we would like to speak to someone in cloning."

"That's a restricted ward. Not just anyone can come and clone himself or herself."

"Of course not. Ridiculous. Clones of *us*? Good god, that'd be horrible. We're here to ask on behalf of Vice Admiral Dickless (by the way, your circumcision ward did fine work on the removal of his genitalia!) whether or not you can clone a heterosexual daughter for him. The press, as you know, has been merciless to his poor lesbian daughter."

"Poor?" screeched Nan. "Do you know how much money that family has? Enough to build a whole new ward for the hospital and a recreation center for the staff. That *is* what the Vice Admiral was talking about, wasn't he?"

"Yes, but that's not to be discussed!" scolded Sam, trying to come across as the boss. "We just need a quick tour of the facilities."

"Well, we don't have any guides..."

"Not to worry. We'll just discreetly show ourselves around. We won't get in the way. We'll only be a half-hour or so."

"Did you say a recreation center for staff?"

"No, we didn't. Sh!" said Sam, winking.

"Okay, then, but a half hour only. After that I have to call security. We're not supposed to allow any unauthorized visitors."

"Oh, we're authorized. The Vice Admiral is in such a hurry, though, that we had to forego the traditional red tape this time. He couldn't spare the extra two weeks."

"I know what you mean. Okay, go ahead then," she said, and she returned to her registration files.

"Quick! Come on," said Nin.

"Right behind you," said Nan.

They went in through the out door of a sealed-off area when an orderly left. They entered a hallway filled with display cases of clone models, and each model was the Emperor. They saw Bulked-up Muscleman Emperor, Super-Tall Basketball Emperor, Darth Emperor, Sumo Emperor, Super-Sized Cranium Emperor, and, for the kids, Fashion Designer Emperor, Army Guy Emperor, Horse Groomer Emperor, Movie Star Emperor. And dozens more. Collect them and trade them with your friends! An entire culture of clones coming soon!

"Any deviation from the Pinocchibush agenda is damned unpatriotic," read a sign on the wall. "You either agree with Pinocchibush, or you are a heathen member of the axis of evil."

Another sign read: "One world, one culture, one mind: Pinocchibush's!"

They read the signs and were appropriately dumb-founded. The room was as quiet as a Cistercian blog.

"This is worse than the ward of toe-stirs," said Nan, finally breaking the silence.

"Or a jar of mixed penis," replied Sam, with a single chuckle.

"Assaulted jar," added Nin, nervously. They located the control center of the room, to which was attached a presumably-cloned brain of the Emperor.

"Okay—there's the brain. Nan, hand me the plastique."

"What if that's the *real* brain," said Sam, "and the rest are clones?"

"I think there'd be better security."

"You're probably right."

"I don't know," said Nan. "It looks like some of the emperors are male, others female, and still others andro-gynous or even hermaphroditic. Maybe this is the sort of advancement needed by society."

"What? You idiot!" answered Nin, placing the plastique at the brainstem. "A fascism of androgyny is still fascism. Approving of dictatorship just because your side would benefit is unconscionable. Remember how the Emperor solidified his power: by staging a mock terrorist attack on the cultural center of the empire. This way he could simul-taneously silence dissident artists while setting the table for an imperialist expansionist war." Click!

"Okay," said Nan.

"Come on," said Nin. "We have ten minutes to get out of here."

From across the field beyond the parking lot, the ex-plosion was beautiful, its plume reaching to heaven for purification and justification, which it received in its dissi-pation.

Fusty, *lis pendens* took my breath away. Would I get it back? That was hard to say.

Breathing had been made illegal in 2004. And canned Pinnochibush air smelled like a killing floor. Polyphemus Pinocchibush staring at a mirror at its own Gorgonish hair, the most evil emperor gormandizing there.

Nin & Nan

Millennium alimentary elementary aluminum laminates the luminous elimination of mellifluous lepidopterists who malign my line of neo-Malthusian malediction while claiming "butterfly" means "flutter by" rather than "butter excrement."

The banana moon fills the cold with emptiness. Driving west, I, my destruction left behind, find myself unfindable; I'll never understand myself, so my reason is gone.

I thought, by throwing myself into politics like Lennon I could stave it off a little. Even he only staved it off briefly.

I thought by focusing outward, my innards would heal themselves. However, what I've found is that, as polluted as I am, the outside is polluted more.

There are the realities of life. Learn them now and decide if you want to continue:

No one will ever really love you. They all have angles and games and needs and desires that pollute the purity of real love.

No one will ever really like you. Only when they have to seem like they do to further themselves in others' eyes will they bother to pretend.

No one will ever really tolerate you. Even your parents and spouse will wish you dead over continuing to have to deal with you. They'll love criminals and charlatans over you. Actually, they'll ascribe criminality and charlatanism to you while praising the integrity of the criminals and charlatans.

Pay them no mind. They want to destroy you, or, as I have said elsewhere, they want to *destory* you.

Here is their message: Hatehatehatehatehate...

I hope you are not overwhelmed by its complexity. They cloak it like Joseph, but it's still hatehatehatehate-hate.

"Nan!" A voice. Nin's. "Come on, snap out of it!" And then, apparently to Sam, Nin said, "Nan's lost in reverie again."

"Oh, yeah?" Nan snatched a bugle out of a passer-by's hand and played about twenty notes of a boisterous call and then stopped.

"What are you doing?" asked Nin.

"There! Now I'm lost in 'Reveille'!"

"Isn't that a ghost town along the extraterrestrial highway near Area 51?" asked Sam.

"Nan's been lost there for years," laughed Nin, climbing up into the truck.

"Here," said Sam, "throw this in the CD player."

"What's this?"

"A book-on-CD about Area 51."

"Who roaded down?" asked Nan.

"I don't know. I snagged it in the hospital as we were walking through."

Nan opened the box, but the Area 51 CD was not inside. Instead, Nan found a CD entitled *Preventive Hysterectomy for Troublesome Female Toddlers*.

The CD argued that early hysterectomy, especially infant hysterectomy, prevented not only potential hygiene problems and infections—the same argument used for circumcision—but also prevented undesirable sexual behavior problems, including emotional upheaval due to hormonal imbalance. Of course, circumcision and excision, or female circumcision, are both prescribed as methods of preventing randiness and nymphomania and other sexual maladies. Thus, argued the CD, preventive hysterectomy was the best way to assure parents of having well-mannered and cooperative daughters.

"Hey," said Sam, after ten minutes. "What's that got to do with Area 51?"

"Maybe the aliens swapped the CDs," answered Nin.

"Maybe we should go back and blow up the rest of the hospital, too," said Nan.

"Are you kidding? We disabled it as much as we can. We now need to put some good distance between us and it," said Sam.

"And then on to the capitol!" said Nin.

"Yes!" agreed Sam.

Chapter Twelve: And Bethagain

"Why not?"

"Oh, come on, Nan. She's probably still pissed about the Dom Perignon on her hotel tab."

"I bet she didn't remember not drinking it herself."

"Maybe, but we need her."

"No, Sam. *You* might need her. I don't."

"Well, just apologize."

"No. I'm going down to the bar to find Nin. You let us know when you're done."

Nan left the hotel room at the casino, amazed that they were back there again. But they'd agreed. They'd hoped Beth could be persuaded to worm her way into Pinocchibush's inner circle. There she could keep an eye on things.

"I'm none the better for the wear and tear on my own old clothes, so ye'd better be keeping to the center lane," said Beth to Sam. And so they talked about her role in an elaborate play designed to humiliate and disgrace Pinocchibush, forcing him at the least to abdicate his throne as had his father, Pinocchiclinton, whose nose grew out of his pants. At least his father had not been an imperialist expansionist working in cahoots with oil companies.

In Beth's hotel room, following her tirade and the ensuing reconciliation with Sam, the television came on, and Pinocchibush's ubiquitous face appeared. Nin and Nan returned.

"The broodish attack on the Makil Health Care Center this afternoon has resorted in one nambatory response on behalf of this excathedra: we have discovered oil in the hill country and must begin drilling immediately to finance our counter-insurrectsurgence effects, er, efforts. We expect our neighbors to lower all braid terriers—"

The Emperor turned his head to the side to hear something shouted to him by someone off-camera—

—"er, trade barriers and open their arms to the flow of our oil..."

"Yuck. What an image," said Sam.

"So he's using the attack as an excuse to mine public lands," said Beth.

"Yeah—*our* public lands," said Nin. "We've got to stop that madman!"

"Shh!" said Nan. "Taximeter cabriolets!"

"To thine taximeter cabriolets?" asked Beth, not understanding. She's braided her hair like a terrier, thought Nin. We've got to change her hair before she enters the capitol.

Crossing the river to the capitol, they were robbed by crook trout. One seemed familiar to Nan. "Wasn't he in *Star Wars*? The country-and-western bad guy, Darth Brooks?"

Nin, not listening, shrugged. All Nin wanted was for all this to be over, to be home again, in the hill, watching satellite TV until boredom brought sleep.

Sam was rehearsing Beth in how to be a sleazy girl. Nan didn't think she needed much coaching.

Nin went over strategy with Sam and Beth—how to enter the capitol, where its weaknesses were, where to penetrate it, and what to do when inside. Nan helped her with her mental sharpening—they played go and chess and skat, worked crosswords and acrostics, and listened to Mozart.

Seduction wouldn't be enough to guarantee a scandal—Beth would have to "bobbitize" the Emperor, after a fashion. Sam began working with her on musical scales and jaw-strengthening exercises. Like a clarinetist, he wanted to fortify her bite.

"No hands!" he'd yell at her. "Hold that note in your teeth! No hands!"

Beth was happy to do her bit for the plan. Her family had been prominent before Pinocchibush had himself coronated Emperor. In the old kingdom, Beth's family had been haberdashers to the king's family. Beth's family's outspokenness against the king's imperialistic plans to annex the poorer nations surrounding the kingdom met with the ire of the king and a dismissal from all official business in the new empire. Beth's maternal side of the family had included three members of parliament, so the Emperor's dissolution of parliament had similarly left that side of the family disenfranchised.

Thus, Beth had stacks of money and an enormous chip on her shoulder. She had been but five years old when her family was kicked out of the inner circle, and she had grown up fixating on her hatred of Pinocchibush.

The Emperor's wrath was growing. He kept appearing on TV, interrupting Nan's favorite TV show, *Daphne the Diabetic Duck-billed Dinosaur*, for sillier and sillier reasons.

"We have decided to curfew instead of many" was announced one day.

"You may be aware that we are not seeing you" was heard as "Naziing you."

Airplanes were being inspected for their "fusel" age.

Public mental health funding was no longer going to be awarded to oxymorons.

Former wards of the court would be rewarded.

The psalter was peppered with profound profanation.

Anachronistic anarchists would be executed by hang-fire.

All watchmakers were to be arrested under suspicion of aiding and abetting on escaped cockfights.

"No clone could ever be that stupid," said Nin. "He's got to be the real one. I know we can get to him at the TV studio."

Chapter Thirteen: TV

The key grip was wagering with the gaffer when our heroes waltzed into Western Sitcom Town.

Jingle jangle. "Howdy, strangers. What brings you to Western Sitcom Town?" asked a sheriff.

Sam put on a Sam Spade accent and said, "We've got you dead to rights, law man. Where are you keeping the talking heads?"

"Oh. You want the talk show and news sets. Studio 13."

"Don't say a word about this to anyone, go it? Or you'll be sleepin' with the fish and chips. Got it?" Then Sam patted the sheriff's paunch and walked off, the others following.

"Why antagonize him? We could have blown it!" demanded Nan outside.

"No. He's used to making his will subservient to that of a superior. All we had to do was show him *we* were superior and he caved. It's easy. It's basic personality disruption."

"It's messing with people. Remember—you're not supposed to mess with people or you'll get hurt."

"Thanks, Televangelist."

"At least I have no guilt," said Nan.

"Oh, yeah? Where's the money, then?"

"Back up in the hills with the Indians," said Nan.

"Very funny. Anyway, that was no regular sheriff. It was just an android."

"He could be saying the same thing about you."

"Sam, I think that was an authentic actor," said Beth.

"There's no such thing, babe. They're all androids."

"Oh, so you were saying *actors* make themselves subservient?"

Sam shrugged.

"Sheriffs?"

Sam shrugged again. "Both. Most people, as far as I can tell, are androids. That's how Pinocchibush took over so easily. They are easily duped."

"And we nuts bolted," said Nan.

"Beth, the Emperor is due to arrive in a half-hour. You go ahead, and we'll wait in the commissary."

Beth went ahead to Studio 13. Her fake ID stated that she was an intern.

Surprisingly, the Emperor's dressing room had been left unguarded. It took little effort for her to change into the guise of a chambermaid—they had heard that the Emperor favored them—and hide inside the wardrobe, waiting for his arrival.

Finally, after an eternity of nervous breathing, Beth relaxed, and the wardrobe opened.

The Emperor, as expected, was alone, and he took the bait. He was an odd man in intimacy, Beth discovered, and he wanted her upside down and astride his nose atop the divan. With a bite and a twirl, the Emperor's lower appendage was severed and his mouth duck-taped shut. She taped him to the divan and, with a second, unplanned bite, she bit off the other offending appendage in the middle of his face.

Both of these she took up and quickly flushed down

the toilet. She washed her face, changed her clothes, climbed onto the veranda, reentered the building through another window and, before anything was noticed, she, Sam, Nin and Nan were leaving the commissary and walking towards their waiting vehicle. Beth was enjoying an egg salad sandwich that she had purchased from a vending machine in the commissary. The mustard washed the taste of Pinocchibush out of her mouth.

It was not the loss of the lower appendage that eventually proved Pinocchibush's undoing. Of course, rumors of the deed spread rapidly throughout the Empire, and the "Emperor without a Staff" became a pet joke in international diplomatic circles.

Actually, it was the loss of the other appendage that undid the Empire.

The people of the Empire had been able to tolerate their jackass of an emperor so long as they could easily tell when he was lying or if he was being truthful (and, to be fair, there had been a handful of occasions of the latter). What, however, they found intolerable, was not knowing. And without his growing appendage, his word became suspect, which was worse than being ridiculed for lying. One can deal with a liar. One cannot deal with a person who is unpredictable. Within a few weeks, members of the inner circle, now completely paranoid because they could no longer read the Emperor, conspired against him and had him poisoned in his bed. So many claims to leadership ensued that the Empire fell apart into its natural divisions, and life as it had been before once again resumed.

Nin & Nan

Nin and Nan returned to their hill, alarmed to see the road rebuilt and a new billboard being erected. For the moment, however, they decided not to do anything about it at all.